Corinna Rogers

I've always wanted to tell stories for a living and I can't stand the idea that the only great story to be told in romance is will-they-or-won't-they – especially when there's a whole other world to explore through the looking glass once they do finally get together! Exploring the unseen side of relationships, exploring what makes characters special when they're in awful situations, exploring how a book can grab you and refuse to let you go – those are the passions that drive my storytelling. I love world-building, I love language, and I love hearing people speak about something that makes them truly passionate. I love books that you can fall into like comfortable furniture, and trust them to take you for a ride through haunted woods. I want people to feel challenged and delighted rather than simply amused and distracted. I believe in the power of entertainment, and I hope to share some of the stories and characters that live in my mind.

Having studied, lived and taught in California, New York, London and Japan, I now live in North Carolina with the love of my life and too many cats.

If you would like to find out more about me and my books, you can follow me on Twitter @Corinna_Rogers.

Flameborn

Mortals & Myths Book Two

CORINNA ROGERS

A division of HarperCollins*Publishers*
www.harpercollins.co.uk

Harper*Impulse* an imprint of
HarperCollins*Publishers*
1 London Bridge Street
London SE1 9GF

www.harpercollins.co.uk

A Paperback Original 2016

First published in Great Britain in ebook format by Harper*Impulse* 2016

A catalogue record for this book
is available from the British Library

ISBN: 9780008115616

Clays Ltd, St Ives plc

Find out more about HarperCollins and the environment at
www.harpercollins.co.uk/green

Chapter One

Fire lances out of the building, propelled not by physics but by the deft hand of a monster with a plan. Drake moves, but he's too late for the swift arc of flame, for the way it reaches out for him, lashing in a broad arc, the heat searing his lungs even from this distance.

A hand grabs his arm, yanking him back to safety. *Right. I have a partner.*

That simple thought spurs Drake into action. He leaps forward, unsheathing the sword from his back and charging towards the burning building. It's fine to be a little reckless, he tells himself, because there's someone to watch his back.

The Inferna has taken up residence in a shitty motel, operating out of Room 183. Grumbling that it should at least have the decency to be in Room 666, Drake draws back and slams his foot into the door, splintering the wood as he dives to the side to make sure he doesn't get hit by the blast.

When no blast follows, he blinks for a second. The door is off its hinges; a fierce wind whips sideways, yanking the fire away from him and saving him from the scorching that would have been a bitch to heal. Not only that, but an Inferna's flames are never just fire. If any one of those had hit him, he'd be feeling a lot more than a horrendous burning sensation, which means the wind is also magical. He turns his head and catches the barest glimpse of a familiar face, tense in concentration.

"Go!"

Drake nods. They both know what it's like, fighting for time when there isn't any. The first step inside the motel is confusing, heat at his front, cold wind at his back, but then the hot air buffets him and he has a hell of a lot more to worry about.

Opening his eyes is always harder inside a burning building, and Drake would give almost anything not to know that so well. They water in less than a second, and the sound of the wind behind him is second only to the creaking, breaking beams of the motel itself. "Cheap plywood and plaster," he calls over his shoulder, throwing an arm over his mouth before he tries to breathe. The heat of the air sears his lungs, no matter how much of it is whipped away from him by the wind. "It's going up fast, so look hard!"

"I can't keep the wind on you and look magically at the same time," Shane shouts back. "Get out for a second."

Drake hesitates and a beam falls. He barely rolls to the side in time, reflexively patting himself down to make sure his heavy denim and flannel haven't caught fire yet. A spark tries to start in his beard and he swats it out, hardly feeling the prickle of pain.

"Go! You're wasting time!"

Reason tells Drake that he has to leave, has to let Shane do his thing, because he's the only one who can find the creature fast enough. If they put the fire out, the Inferna will simply disappear, bursting into life at a new location with a new set of lungs to breathe out the flame. Judging by the state of the motel, Drake hazards that they have four, maybe five, minutes until the whole thing comes crumbling down.

Still, instinct makes him hesitate. Shane might be able to find the creature on his own, but dealing with it is a different story. Inferna are strong, and—

Shane whacks him in the head, turning to physically kick him back out the door. The long boots he wears are heavy, even without the force of a grown man's kick. Drake takes the blow easily, but catches sight of Shane's exasperated, worried face. "Fine!" he shouts, and ducks out the door.

Time passes much more slowly when he's not in the thick of the action. It wears on him, pacing back and forth outside the crumbling building, able to do nothing but wait. He tries taking a peek through one window, but even getting that close is dangerous. One of the windows near him shatters, glass exploding outwards, and Drake doesn't take the chance that the one he's looking through will do the same thing.

From outside, all he can see is a sphere of white light. It's difficult to make out in the midst of all the flames, but Drake manages to keep his eyes on it. A slow swirl of magic emanates from it in a way he can feel in his bones, at least when he's in contact with the sword he holds. Every instinct he has tells him to run inside, to find the culprit, to make sure everything is fine. That's what he does, after all, and to be stuck on the outside looking in…

It's anathema.

The light suddenly streaks across the room, cleaving through a wall. Drake runs left, following the light with his eyes. Shane wouldn't move like that unless he'd found something, he reasons, and breaks the next door open with a full-body slam. He draws the sword, feeling the sweet peace of its blade surround him, and charges into the unrelenting flames.

The world splits.

Part of him is still present, fighting through the flames. Drake feels his body moving, muscles cording under the skin as he dashes in, scanning the burning motel for the Inferna's presence. Shane had moved, so it has to be close. There—a dark blob, like a sunspot against the orange tongues of flame, darts first to the left, then to the right, evading Shane's strikes.

The other part of Drake is anything but present.

Every gust of heat takes him farther away, showing him not the motel in front of his eyes, but memories. They don't make sense, not all at once, but the gasping surges of fire drive him out of reality and into his mind all the same.

He'd stumbled into an Inferna lair once, in his late teens. Even that memory sends him back. Shane had been a few steps behind when Drake had tripped, stumbling into a hole as they searched for their bounty. The Inferna's cave had exploded into flames, and Drake had found himself on a roller coaster with his mother, laughing at his father and sister, afraid of heights on the ground. Moments later, Shane had pulled him free, slapping his face, and it had taken long days for Drake to recover from the intensity of that memory.

Bright white light gleams suddenly, slicing through the flames as well as any wind could have. Shane's light is blue and on the other side of the room; the light that deals with the Inferna's magic comes from the sword in Drake's hand, sanctified magic protecting him from the worst effects of inhuman magic. The memories still flood him—

"You're such a dork!" his sister Clara laughs, and moves to sit with her friends on the school bus, even on her first day of school.

—Drake remembers where he is, and he can still move.

A sudden burst of wind and light from Shane manages to isolate the Inferna. Drake's long legs carry him close, and the creature spits out fire—

"Why isn't your last name Nelson?"

"They're just foster parents. It'd be Cooper-Walker-Jones-Remmington-Nelson by now."

—Drake takes the blast full force and hears himself let out a noise like a roar when he breaks through, slamming the sword through the creature's writhing body, pinning it to the wall. It tries to climb up the blade, but Drake doesn't let go, lashing out with a foot to slam it back to the wall, ignoring the—

Shane's touch, his lips ghosting down over Drake's spine, his voice ragged and needy, begging, hands urgent, teeth sharp—

—Drake yanks the sword free and spins, using his body weight to drive his next slice home.

The Inferna's head rolls slowly away from its body, now sad and corporeal. It shrivels down to a coal, the inner light dying out and leaving nothing but a wrinkled skin over charred black insides. Drake exhales deeply and sheathes the sword on his back. It's a quick draw, less than a second from the impulse of danger to the sword being in his hand and ready to use, and keeping his hands free has saved his life more times than wandering around with a drawn sword has. "Clear?" he yells, hoping Shane can hear him.

"All clear," the call comes back. Shane peels himself away from the wall and drapes over a fallen beam. He coughs, then inhales deeply, magic tingeing the air in front of his nostrils, and breathes out deeply this time, with no trace of a wheeze. "You need an inhaler?"

Drake shakes his head. "Sword protected me. It doesn't snap back like that." He does feel his usual aches and pains now, the ones that come with age and a lifetime of being beaten up that are suppressed by the power the sword gives him. He nudges the coal of the Inferna's body with a toe and it starts crumbling. "They seem like they're getting stronger to you lately?"

"Maybe you're just getting slower, old man," Shane teases, and makes as if to come over and stand next to him. He thinks better of it a second later, heading for the door instead. "You get singed in that first charge, baby?"

"Got worse from the stove." A glint of light in the center of the coals catches his eye and Drake grimaces. "Hold up, this one might still be alive. Lemme stomp it out."

"That's a little cruel. Let it skulk back to its master. Maybe we can follow it."

Drake kicks the coal a little harder and it fractures into halves, then a dozen pieces when each half hits the ground, the size of a luggage carry-on when it's split. At the center, a deep orange-red glow pulses and ebbs, startlingly bright in the center of the coals, like concentrated fire made liquid. "I've never seen anything like this," he says. "I've cracked open a lot of Inferna."

"Probably not as many as I have."

Drake raises an eyebrow and Shane shrugs, coming to kneel next to the coals. "I *did* work for the Fire Queen's mortal enemy for ten years."

"I thought they were husband and wife."

"Pretty sure they're brother and sister, too. Doesn't mean they aren't mortal enemies."

Drake snorts and prods the Inferna's corpse with the toe of his boot. The liquid sticks to his boot for a moment, more like gel than anything, and then slowly detaches and slides back into the coal. If it weren't for the changing play of colors, there'd be no reason to think it's alive, much less that it's some part of the Inferna itself. They're small, but Drake has never had a problem with seeing them as creatures of flesh and blood before they burn away to coal. He sighs and stands up. "Can you freeze it or something? It's bothering me and I'm not sure stomping will help."

Shane shrugs and points a finger. A thin stream of water swirls out of the air, soaking the coals, and has no effect on the little pool whatsoever.

"Uh…"

Shane flushes hot, frowns, and points again, more firmly this time. Another jet swirls down, this one freezing as it does, though just enough that a few ice crystals form in the middle of the water. At this, the liquid flinches, glows for a moment, then settles.

"I think your finger is broken."

"It's not supposed to do that!" Shane stares down at his own hand, then turns and stalks out of the burned-out motel, cursing to himself and shaking his hand out at the wrist.

"Don't worry," Drake calls, a hint of a grin in his voice. "Happens to every guy as you get older."

"Fucking suck my dick!"

Drake laughs, and in the second he turns his head to watch Shane slam what's left of the door, the liquid fire moves. He sees it out of the corner of his eye, but not fast enough to get a hand on his sword. His mind misfires, going for a reaction that won't get him killed, and comes up blank for the first time in years.

They'd had a code, back when they'd first started hunting down the magical creatures that preyed on those less able to defend themselves. They'd sworn it then, in blood and when looking in each others' eyes. *"No matter what, we keep it from getting out into the world if we can help it."*

Drake throws himself sideways as the liquid fire streaks towards the door, and if his size is good for little else it's at least good when he wants to act like a barrier. Out the door is where Shane is, Drake remembers just in time, and opens his mouth to call.

The fire darts sideways at the last second, neatly zapping itself down his throat, and Drake almost blacks out from the pain. He would scream, if screaming didn't involve his throat. He throws himself back violently, slamming his back to the wall with the last bit of his conscious effort, trying to dislodge whatever it is in a haze of blinding, searing pain. The fire feels like it looks, which is no consolation; searing fire made liquid feels a hell of a lot like a huge gulp of boiling oil, and Drake can feel his insides roasting more every millisecond. His lungs lock up, unable to function when something tears its way through him. He only has a fleeting second to wonder whether the creature will burn a hole out or be suffocated inside his corpse when warm hands clutch his face.

It would be nice to have his face be the last thing I see, Drake thinks dimly. It's the only thought that registers through the pain, through the smell of his own melting insides, but forcing his eyes open is a hundred, a thousand, times harder than usual. He can feel every slide of the creature in his throat, every frantic wriggle, and as a vague plan to suffocate it Drake closes his jaw as his last act of defiance.

Something long and cool presses into the palm of his hand, and Drake's eyes snap open.

The sword in his hand blazes, pressed there by Shane's hands around his, and the light from the sword envelops his body. Everywhere it touches, it seals, making his flesh stronger, making his body hardier, and Drake almost lets out a sob of relief when the pain starts to fade. He tries to take a breath and his lungs slowly, begrudgingly, start working. The first gulp of air banishes the firespots on his vision, and the second makes him feel like he's not actually dead, something he considers pretty helpful.

Drake's fingers close around the sword without Shane's help, squeezing it tightly for the salvation it is. The creature is still inside him, thrashing around, and Drake doesn't dare let go.

"—Got to open up for me, baby, let me see the damage. You need to *call* me before you start doing idiot things like—"

Shane has been talking for a while, Drake realizes, and has to wonder whether he'd passed out after all.

"Swallowed it." He'd expected his voice to be a raw rasp of a thing, but it sounds as normal as ever to his own ears. "It came at the door. I didn't know what to do."

Shane's laughter borders on the hysterical. "Oh, *now* your first impulse is to swallow."

"Shane."

"Sorry, sorry, but don't expect that joke to die any time soon. Is it still…"

Drake grimaces. "It's still in me. Gimme your hand."

He grabs Shane's hand with the one not clutching the sword, and brings it to his own belly. Shane lets out a startled curse and yanks his hand away. "It's—it's hot!"

"Having any more luck with that ice?"

Shane makes a face at him and helps him off the floor, where he'd apparently fallen without realizing it. "Not sure what's up. Might have something to do with being so close to a bunch of fire."

"Never stopped you before. I've seen you make fires when you were surrounded by ice."

"Yeah. It's probably to do with the Ice King. Maybe he took that away from me. Pretty small revenge for destroying his palace and murdering all of his servants, but maybe he's also a petty son of a bitch."

"Wouldn't you know if he is?" It's a delicate question. Drake isn't sure how much Shane really doesn't remember and how much he's just repressing because he doesn't want to remember it. Honestly, knowing even a small fraction of the things Shane had done in the Ice King's service, he can't say he blames him.

Shane hesitates, then shakes his head, kicking what's left of the door off its hinges. "I don't remember much of that time, you know. Plus, I'm pretty sure we weren't exactly best friends. Even when I was his number one, I was still scared as hell of him, back when I still had fear. Can you walk?"

"Nothing wrong with me." At least, nothing feels wrong. The sturdy truck Drake bought second-hand to replace the SUV that had flipped on him is a wide older model, but neither of them blink at it when they hop into the cab. Drake gets in a bit more carefully than Shane, on the passenger's side, and carefully lays the sword diagonally across his lap.

"Not sure I'm real comfortable with this," Shane admits. "What if I hit a bump and you impale yourself?"

"What if you don't drive like an asshole? Besides, I'm a lot less fond of some flaming slug eating its way through my intestines."

"Yeah, it might damage the upholstery if it gets out. You need to go by the Church?"

Drake chews on his bottom lip for a minute, thinking. "I'd

better. The sword is working really well against it, better than most things. I might be able to get something out of Father Aaron there."

"I bet you will," Shane mutters.

Drake shuts his mouth, clenching his jaw shut. There's nothing good he can say to that comment that won't start a fight, and both of them know it. Shane has never liked Father Aaron, but Drake had always assumed it was some natural aversion to the Church in general. It hasn't abated since he got his soul back, however, and the idea that he'll just have to accept this animosity rubs Drake the wrong way.

Shane pulls jerkily out into the street, amid unhelpful tips from Drake about how to handle the stick shift. At least he doesn't stall at the intersection this time, which Drake decides to consider a small win. "You want me to wait in the car?"

"You don't like it inside."

Shane's hands tighten on the steering wheel and his voice is tight when he speaks. "That wasn't me. You *know* that. Christ, why are we still even having this conversation?"

Drake gives him a sideways look, then focuses on the road so he doesn't lose his temper. Shane might not remember all that well, but Drake had lived through that decade and remembers it plenty for the both of them. "You're saying you want to come in and talk to Father Aaron?"

Shane almost swerves into traffic and Drake grips the sword as tightly as he can. "Is there some way I can avoid going in *and* avoid you being alone with him?"

"Why don't you want me alone with him?"

"Nothing against him, I just don't like you hanging out with guys that want to bone you into next week."

Drake's eyebrows shoot straight up and he turns, incredulous, to stare at Shane's clenched jaw, his fingers tight on the wheel. Whatever reply he'd been about to make fades on his tongue. Shane is a lot of things—irrational, flighty, over-eager, occasionally petty—but he's not jealous for no reason. At least, he hasn't been in the past, Drake reminds himself.

Not for the first time, he has to wonder how much of the boy he'd loved is in the man driving the truck.

"He's a priest," he says quietly, trying not to dismiss Shane's feelings just because he thinks (knows) they're ridiculous. "Even if he had some weird thing for me—which I really don't think he does—"

"He does."

"*Even if*, he's still got his vows." Drake carefully transfers the grip of his sword to his right hand and reaches the left over to squeeze Shane's shoulder. "I'm flattered you think I'm hot enough to turn a priest, but seriously."

Shane takes his eyes off the road for longer than Drake is entirely comfortable with, then grins. "Because you're all mine, right?"

There's something about the way he says it—relief, pride, pleasure—that makes Drake's expression soften. "Yeah. Feels good to say it again."

"Yeah, well, talk is cheap." Shane's hand tightens on his and yanks it down, pressing Drake's palm between his legs as he drives with one hand.

"Um?" Drake looks from the road to Shane's hand to his face, searching for something besides cocky good humor and finding nothing. "Jesus, you hedonist, wait until we get home."

"Don't wanna. You know fighting always makes me hard."

"That's your problem."

"Always makes you hard, too."

"That's my problem. Dammit, concentrate on the road!"

"Road isn't going anywhere. Come on, baby, your hand feels so good. I love the calluses and how strong you are. Feel how hard I am."

It's hard not to. Shane's cock throbs under Drake's hand, even through the denim of his jeans. Drake swallows hard, fingers curling in spite of himself. Shane's not wrong, and that's a problem. Fighting does usually make him more than eager to fuck, but there've been too many years when he wasn't able to indulge those desires. "I've gotten better at holding it in," he grumbles.

"You're not exactly pulling away." One hand on the steering wheel, Shane flicks open his jeans with the other, enough to make it obvious he's wearing nothing underneath. In spite of himself, Drake swallows hard, mouth gone dry.

Shane lets out a sigh that turns into a groan. "You have about five seconds to stop looking like you're gonna eat it, or I'm going to pull the truck over and—"

"Pull the truck over."

Drake barely has enough time to think frantically, *I meant at an intersection!* before Shane swerves sideways, pulling roughly parallel to the curb and braking hard. The car is still lurching when Shane grabs his face, kissing him fiercely until they're both flushed, sucking Drake's bottom lip into his mouth to scrape his teeth across it and make them both groan.

"Every time," Drake mutters, fingers flexing on the sword he can't goddamn put down as he rearranges his position. "You're so damn *needy* whenever we get into a good fight."

"After," Shane corrects, and pulls himself out of his jeans. He's obviously achingly hard, and Drake's own cock gives a twitch in his pants at the sight. "God, you look like you want it. Only takes a near-death experience to make you act like a slut, huh?"

"Shut up." Drake bends, sliding his lips around the head of Shane's cock, eyes fluttering closed at the taste. He swipes the flat of his tongue over it, and Shane grips the steering wheel, a hand coming to tangle in his hair, pushing him down without any pretense, without any apology.

Drake doesn't want pretenses and apologies. He wants the slick, musky scent dragging over his tongue, the soft skin over hard muscle stretching his lips, the sound of Shane panting heavy and quick in his ears.

"You act," Shane says, and gasps occasionally when Drake scrapes his teeth gently, "like I n-never let you do this, fuck."

Drake pulls off for a second, letting the swollen head rub against his lips, sticky and slippery with his spit, so hard it quivers against him. "You're usually too eager to jump on my dick."

"Uh-uh," Shane teases. His hand grips Drakes hair tighter, not letting him up again. "You can't dirty-talk me like I'm the slut when you're practically inhaling my dick. God, you must be gagging for it."

Shane is the one that gets off on dirty talk. Usually, Drake is only too happy to oblige him, shoving him over a table and nailing him into next week, and Shane gets off on every second of it, but now…

Now, he's having a hard time denying just how much he likes having it in his mouth. It's stupid to try, when his own cock is trying to drill a hole through his jeans just from the taste of Shane's dripping all over his tongue, making it slippery and forcing sloppy, messy noises out of his mouth with every thrust.

Shane doesn't move his hips much when he's getting blow-jobs, Drake knows, even if it's been a hell of a long time since he's had his mouth around it. Long fingers tighten in his hair, and Drake tries to relax, letting Shane move his head up and down, the thick head pressing at the back of his throat, the taste everywhere in his nose. Even now, there's the dark urge to grab Shane by the throat, to flip him over and take him rough and hard, to slap him around a little until he comes all over himself.

They've always been a little fucked up.

Drake curls his tongue around the length, sucking hard and long, his fingers coming up to knead into Shane's thigh.

"That's it, baby," Shane grunts, letting his legs splay farther apart. "I know you're dick-hungry as hell right now—yeah, just like that, shit, you've got a slutty tongue for such a respectable guy." His voice is fond, heavy-laden with arousal and that same hunger, and a tenseness that means he's got to be almost there. He laughs, a hitching breath, and warns, "You better clean it up real good, or you're gonna be going into your precious church with come in your beard."

You bastard.

Drake starts to pull off, probably to growl and snap at Shane, but Shane's hand is strong in this position and holds him down hard. That thick cock bumps the back of his throat one more time, and Shane sucks in a breath, yanking back on his hair, the *asshole*.

Wet heat floods Drake's mouth, spilling over his tongue in thick, bitter ropes. Drake tries not to gag, breathing through his nose and grabbing at Shane's jeans, hand curling into a fist as he tries to choke it down. He manages a couple mouthfuls, then pulls off when Shane's hand goes limp, coughing and scrubbing at his mouth with the back of his hand. "You fucking asshole," he croaks, voice hoarse as his hand comes away wet.

Shane shrugs. "Not my fault you're such a bad gay. I like the taste of yours just fine."

"Mine tastes better! You eat all that junk food shit, no wonder."

Shane laughs, then reaches out and grabs Drake's hand, bringing it up to his own lips. Slowly, holding Drake's eyes the whole time, he runs his tongue up through the sticky smear on his hand, grinning when he gets to the end of it, and swallows. Drake's cock makes a valiant attempt to punch its way out of his jeans. "I think I taste just fine."

"Shane." Drake's voice is hoarse and needy, and Shane just rolls his eyes. "Of course, baby."

Half a second later Drake has to wonder if Shane used magic to get his cock out that quickly. His mouth is searingly hot, tongue lashing against his length, and Drake's head tips back against the car's seat. "Now who's the one with a slutty tongue?"

Shane pulls off, delicately tracing the slit at the end of Drake's cock. "Yeah, I'm pretty sure it's always me. Fuck my face, I want you to shoot it down my throat."

"I just bet you do." The sentence turns into a groan when Shane dives down, taking him all in, swallowing around the thick length of Drake's cock, making his balls ache from being so ready. "Jesus, just—you fucking whore, I'm going to throw you onto every surface you've ever *seen* later—"

Shane looks up at him, eyes dilated, lips stretched wide, shiny and wet from the drool and precum coating his face, and Drake loses it. He humps up frantically into Shane's mouth, holding him down with one hand, thrusting deep into his throat over and over again, bruising those pretty lips. All so Shane can feel how hard he is, how much he *wants*.

The sudden impulse to pull out and come all over Shane's face is so strong, Drake almost gives in. Only the thought that they're going into the church in a second gives him pause and he lets out a frustrated noise, slamming his cock so deep down Shane's throat that he can hear Shane choke for the first time. Then everything goes white, bursting behind his eyelids, pleasure exploding through his body when he comes long and hard down Shane's throat.

For a long time, Drake isn't aware he's breathing. The only sounds in the cabin are Shane's breaths, ragged and labored and a little panicky towards the end, until he slaps Drake's wrist. "Huh? Oh, sorry."

Shane pulls off with a gasp as soon as Drake removes his hand, wiping his streaming eyes with his thumbs, coughing a little. "Rude."

"You like it."

Shane punches him in the arm, not exactly gentle. "Still rude. Maybe I shouldn't tell you what's in your beard."

Drake pulls the mirror down from above the passenger's side window, scrutinizing his face closely.

"Kidding."

Drake gives him a glare, noting the marked lack of blotchy redness in Shane's face. He's used to seeing Shane use magic for big things—he'd seen him re-grow an entire hand once, though that had been when his powers had been augmented by the Ice King—but the tiny casual displays are the ones that make him nervous. Of course, those are the things that Shane had concealed from him before, for exactly that reason. *Flashy Mages don't live as long*, he'd said years ago, but seems to have dropped that concern.

Drake shrugs off the uncomfortable thought, twisting to open the door with his left hand, right still firmly gripping the sword's hilt. If it weren't for the boost of endurance and power the sword lends him, he'd probably be feeling his fingers cramping by now.

"How long are you gonna hold it?" Shane asks, mind obviously running along the same lines as they climb the stone steps.

"Until I figure out how to get the damn thing out of me."

"That's gonna be awkward if we want to go out to dinner."

"With what money?"

Shane makes a face at that, but doesn't argue. "Your fingers are gonna freeze that way. At least they'll be stuck in a shape that's easy to—"

"*Not* in church, Shane."

That earns him an eyeroll as Shane tosses back his hair, letting it shimmer into blue-green waves, hanging just past his shoulders in the back, rippling with magic as it changes color. "Not that guy anymore, Drake. Quit forgetting."

It isn't easy to forget when a little slip-up could mean losing everything he's finally regained, but Drake tries to remember. He reaches for the door, but Shane is there first, eyes fixed on the high vaulted ceilings.

The church is anything but ostentatious, for a big stone building. All mentions of saints, kings, and angels have been removed, leaving empty recesses in the stone where statuary used to reside. Only two pews remain, kept near the back for the disabled and anyone who can't physically stand for more than an hour at a time. The windows aren't made of the glass they look like, but crystalline, and reinforced with plexiglass. Drake isn't entirely sure what denomination the building used to belong to, not that it matters much.

Shane breathes in deeply through his nose, exhaling with a long sigh. "I can't believe I hated this place," he says, eyes half-lidded, fingers twitching. "The air in here is fantastic."

"Seriously? You used to say you couldn't breathe in here."

Shane blinks. "Really? Huh. Must be… hmm." He flicks his tongue out a couple times, rubs the pads of his fingertips together, and frowns. "Yeah, there's magic in here. Like, not just in use, but in the air itself. You can feel it, right?"

"The only kind of magic I can feel is when the sword wants me to kill it. Don't forget I'm just an ordinary human."

"That's an awful and untrue thing to say about yourself! You've seen wonders and horrors humans never have, you've fought false gods and kings and monsters."

"You think that makes me less human?"

Shane gives him a thoughtful look, then deliberately shrugs. "I think it makes you more something else."

Drake shifts uncomfortably, looking around for any trace of Father Aaron or one of his junior priests, anyone that could put a stop to this conversation. Shane had never said things like that before his ordeal, before they'd been separated. "I'm just as human as I ever was. I just have a fancy sword and a magic boyfriend."

It sets off an old worry in him to hear Shane talking like that. He'd wondered a hundred times, before, if Shane would ever get sick of his pet human and find someone better, someone stronger, more powerful. It's possible that just a human isn't enough for Shane anymore, not after everything he's done, every-thing he's been.

The Church only has one bell, a mournful, serious brass bell that Drake knows all too well. It rings now, one deep, penetrating note that always sets Drake's teeth on edge. He looks around just in time to see a junior priest, Father Thomas, he thinks, scurrying for the door before it's thrown open by Father Aaron.

"Champion!"

Father Aaron is a trim man in his forties, with a shock of thick black hair and a deep- bronze complexion. At least, Drake is fairly certain he's in his forties, since he looks almost the same as he had ten years ago. He felt younger then, though, even though there are still no wrinkles around his eyes and mouth, and he doesn't move any more slowly. His back is straight, perfectly so, and long-fingered hands lace together in front of the stark black of his robes. "We ring the bell in joyous celebration, that our Champion has returned." Despite the severity of his demeanor, there's a warmth in his dark eyes that Drake finds comforting.

"I'll just bet you do."

"Shane."

Father Aaron's eyes flick over to Shane, and now lines do appear at the corners of his mouth. He wrestles with himself for a moment, obviously trying to decide whether to avoid conflict or seek it out, and then swallows hard around the impulse and just ignores him instead. "Have you been victorious in your battle, my Champion?"

"He's not *your* anything—"

"I have, Father. We slew the Inferna before it could claim further lives."

Father Aaron finally turns fully away from Shane and frowns, eyes searching as he steps forward. He lays a hand on Drake's head, though he has to reach significantly upwards to do it, and Drake pretends he can't hear Shane grinding his teeth. "Why so much energy?" Father Aaron wonders aloud. "Why do you hold the sword even now? Surely you aren't expecting an attack from those you keep safe."

"I was… injured, Father. This is the only thing that stopped the creature from consuming me whole."

Dismay spreads over the priest's features, and the hand on Drake's hair gets stronger, more possessive. "I have heard," he says carefully, "that the partner you chose once more in life despite all wishes of the Church—"

"Who is standing right here. Geez, you people wonder why no one wants to join you."

"—has some skill in healing." Father Aaron's voice is cool and humorless. "Is he unwilling to save your life?"

"I, uh, don't think he can."

"Ah, so he is merely incompetent rather than cruel. I am relieved to hear that he is at your side in these difficult battles."

Drake's expression hardens. "I'm finding precious little of the Church's blessed forgiveness in you, Father. You and yours want me to be your guardian against the night. That's fine, but that doesn't give you any right to govern my choices."

"No, sadly." Father Aaron gives him a small, sad smile and withdraws his hand. "I just personally think you have abominable taste."

"Which I'm pretty sure is none of your concern," Drake responds evenly. "Can you help me out with the fire slug in my gut, or what?"

Shane nudges his arm, not-so-subtly. "Ask him if we're getting paid," he stage-whispers.

"The position of Champion of the Church is a vaunted, highly-respected, *volunteer* position," Father Aaron snaps, "and occasionally, some of our flock choose to generously contribute in a monetary sense to the care and upkeep of the Champion's generous—"

"So we're *not* getting paid."

"You aren't getting anything," Father Aaron says firmly. "You are not affiliated with us, and we do not beg for you. Our *Champion*, however—"

"What's his is mine, and what's mine is his." Shane starts to step forward, challenging with every flash of his eyes and every movement of his shoulders, and Drake flings out a hand to push him back. He falls back easily, which almost makes Drake angrier. Shane *knows* this is wrong, and he still does it, still pushes those buttons, as if he has no other choice.

"I will make you wait outside again," he warns, and Shane settles slightly. He isn't exactly mollified, but Drake is willing to settle for a lack of current intent to harm. "Father, I do hate to ask, but it's been a rough month for me, financially."

Father Aaron's face softens. "Of course, Champion. I'll pass the basket for you at tomorrow's service. Stick around after we're finished."

Drake isn't especially fond of Father Aaron's sermons, but the idea of being able to pay rent on time is an attractive one. "I'll be grateful, Father. Uh, any idea if there's anything the Church can do about the thing eating me whole? Besides talk about how my boyfriend should be able to fix me?" Against his better judgment, he does sort of enjoy the way Father Aaron flinches whenever he says "boyfriend."

The priest's lips thin. "It's stopped by the sword, which is good. Will you allow me to pray over you?"

Drake hesitates, then nods. "I hope this is one of those prayers with extra juice."

"Nothing less for our Champion."

Drake settles down onto his knees, and Shane abruptly turns and walks away, pacing against one wall in obviously uncomfortable strides. Drake takes a deep breath, finding that peace he usually only sees when he's practicing martial arts, and closes his eyes.

Father Aaron's hand on his head isn't exactly a surprise, but the feeling it brings is. Instead of gentle pressure, there's a soft crackling of power, tamed lightning in every tiny brush of his fingers against Drake's hair. "All-Seeing God," the priest says, bowing his head, "bless your Champion, defender of the flock, he who believes not and fights still. The warrior of your peace has cast his cloak over your undeserving servants. Remove his obstacles, heal his wounds, staunch the flow of his life's blood. Make him whole and well again that he may sacrifice himself in your name, for your pitiful devoted."

Drake winces at the language, but keeps his head bowed. The hand on his head trembles, and white-hot power spills into him, purifying and scouring him from the top down. His stomach turns, and even with the sword in his hand, he can feel the frantic thrashing of the little Inferna creature, thudding against his intestines as the holy fire makes its way down. For a second, he thinks he's imagining the dying screech, but a sharp intake of breath from Father Aaron tells him that it isn't in his head. Drake keeps his eyes squeezed shut, and after a moment, the power scorches through his legs and feet, leaving him shaken, empty, and alive. "Did it work?"

Father Aaron sighs, and withdraws his hand, leaving a tingling, cooling patch on Drake's head. "You truly are still a nonbeliever, aren't you?"

"I'd let you know if that changed." It's not so hard to flash a bit of magic and call a man a god. Drake has seen Shane do more miracles than he's seen from the being behind the Church.

"Have I ever let you down before?"

Drake looks up, meeting his eyes, and says levelly, "Yes."

That at least causes something of a twinge. "Test it yourself. Let go the sword."

I hate faith magic, Drake thinks vehemently. Any time the choice is to trust and possibly die or to stay safe and distrustful, he rarely finds himself on the side of the faithful. He lays the sword on the ground, then carefully, slowly removes his hand.

Nothing sears or flops. His stomach doesn't twist. The usual surge of fatigue hits him, reminding him that his body has human limits even if he can ignore them while he's holding the sword, and old aches so familiar that he rarely feels them make themselves known. Drake exhales deeply, and nods his head. "Thank you, Father."

"Don't thank me. Thank God."

Drake gives a pro forma nod to the ceiling. He's never yet been struck down for not believing, despite being a theoretically important Church person. "Anyway, I'll be back for service tomorrow," he says, rising to his feet with a grimace as he sheathes the sword on his back.

"Before you go…" Father Aaron reaches out a hand, gently grasping Drake's sleeve. "Could we speak in private for a moment?"

"No." Drake raises an eyebrow, and Shane strides over, less repelled by the obvious faith magic. "We're going."

Father Aaron lets out a breath that's closer to a huff, and gives him a truly annoyed glare, which Drake returns placidly. It's a lot easier for the Church to find new priests than new Champions, and unfortunately for Father Aaron, Drake knows it. "You cannot let these fires continue. More and more of us are dying every day."

"If you know where to start looking for her, I'm more than willing to listen." He doesn't have to say who he's talking about. With the Ice King gone from the city, the fires have been closer and closer together, Inferna multiplying, and it's all Drake and Shane can do to keep up.

"I hear the Fire Queen is difficult to find."

"We could have told you that. In fact, we did."

"But she is drawn to those…" Brown eyes flick over to Shane, who takes a half-step back. "Those of her kind."

"Why is it literally always my fault?" Shane doesn't sound terribly perturbed. If anything, his voice is amused. "I'm pretty sure she's not a Mage. Last time I checked I didn't have anywhere near close to the kind of juice she likes throwing around, and I'm the most powerful Mage we've ever met."

"Humility is a virtue—"

"Not one I'm entirely fond of," Shane admits cheerfully. "Not when it's false modesty. I'm the most powerful Mage *you'll* ever meet, that's for sure."

Father Aaron's jaw clenches, and he draws himself up to his full height, which is still a few inches shy of even Shane's. "You have no concept of what I've seen or who I've met. A child like you could never comprehend—"

"I'm older than I look, promise. And better than you seem to think."

"Unless you can tell us where she's hiding," Drake interrupts, stepping none-too-subtly between the two men, "We're going to go find her ourselves. We'll make one of the Inferna talk before dying, eventually."

Father Aaron looks between the two of them, then finally nods, face drawn and less than pleased. "If you ever need to find her, open him up. See what's inside."

Shane grabs the priest by a handful of black fabric, hauling him nearly off the ground. "You little piece of shit, I'm trying to be *civil*," he snarls. "What if I open you up and she shows, huh?"

Father Aaron just blinks at him, unmoved by the words or the display of violence. "Then you'd know that you and I are one and the same. Is that a risk you want to take, Shane Connell?"

"I hate the way you say my name, you goddamned—"

"And we're going." Drake's hand isn't gentle on Shane's shoulder, but it is effective, hauling both of them out of the Church as fast as long legs can carry him, Shane nearly keeping up and having to trot the last few steps.

He doesn't speak for long moments, not until he slides into the driver's seat, sword unbuckled and in the back. His hands tighten on the steering wheel, and he breathes out heavily through his nose, staring straight ahead without seeing much as Shane settles himself into the passenger's seat.

"Well, that was—"

"Not now."

The drive home is silent, save for the occasional clicking of a turn signal and the revving of the motor. Drake pulls up in front of an apartment building that's reasonably shabby for the money (a sign in the window says "Magic and Pets Allowed!"), but doesn't unbuckle his seatbelt.

Shane raises an eyebrow at him. "You're not even coming in? What, just because I grabbed him?"

"You know this is what I'm doing with my life." Drake rubs at the back of his neck, short hairs bristling under his hand. "I'll be home in a few hours. Got a class to teach."

There's something tense and unhappy in Shane's body language as he slides out of the truck. He looks for all the world like he wants to say something, but Drake drives off before he can turn around.

Through the entire drive to the karate studio, Drake feels three things: the dull ache of heat in his lungs, the tingling print of Father Aaron's palm on his head, and the taste of Shane lingering on his lips.

~

Chapter Two

~

Smashing something isn't nearly as much fun when Shane knows he's the one who'll have to pay for it in the long run—or worse, that Drake will have to take late-night classes to pay for it, and that drastically cuts into the time he usually considers "fun." He'd *like* to put his fist through a wall, annoyed at himself, annoyed at priests who don't seem nearly as free from worldly desires as Shane is pretty sure they're supposed to, annoyed at creatures that don't play by the rules when it comes to dying when they're supposed to.

Being a destructive asshole was a lot more fun when he didn't give a shit about the consequences.

Underneath the anger, there's a sulking resentment that it's Friday night and literally no one he knows will want to go out. They'd been *that couple* for a while in their twenties, the ones who rarely went out except with each other, but he had friends. He had people to call up and go clubbing with. Now, with his new "freedom" from the Ice King and ten years down the drain, everyone he knew is either far too involved in their children and work, or have died from a slew of the unnatural causes that normal people like to pretend don't exist.

The ringing of the phone jars him out of his anger, but the sullen, prickling feeling stays. He knows without picking up the phone that it isn't Drake, and grabs the ancient thing off the wall mount. "Yeah?"

"This is a recording. Do not attempt to answer. Your utility bill for this month is past due. Please pay the amount of… One. Hundred. Seventy. Seven. Dollars. And. Fifteen. Cents. By the shut-off date, or your service will be discont—"

He slams the phone down on the stilted voice, then stalks over to the empty coffee can above the fridge, pulling down the change bucket and poking at it with one long finger. The leftovers from Father Aaron's last "payment" glare dully back at him, dirty coins in a lump that fills up half the coffee can and probably isn't anywhere close to being a hundred and seventy-seven bucks.

It wouldn't be the first time they'd gone a month or two without light and heat, and his magic does tend to make that kind of thing a lot more bearable. It's a strain, though, and depletes the power he has available for vaguely important things like fighting bad guys.

And there's rent, and food, and the phone service, and gas for the car…

Shane braces himself, decides that it could be worse, and rifles through the mail to get to a publication he usually throws in the trash, sitting down with a red pen to circle carefully coded jobs that make him feel vaguely greasy to take.

The "MHW," or Magic Help Wanted section of the weekly periodical is never exactly full of winners, but actually flipping through and looking for work makes Shane sort of want to punch himself in the face. The first twenty in a row are all about love potions, something that he's pretty sure doesn't actually exist even if the collective public has decided that if there are Mages now, there *have* to be love potions. He skims the Want Ads, finally landing on a few that aren't about love potions or strange sexual fetishes, and are varying degrees of suspicious.

MHW
STOLEN and LOST MERCHANDISE FIND IT and U GET A CUT

MHW
Emotions, NO LP!!!

MHW
Snakes?!

MHW
I Have Ants, If U Cn Do it Cheaper Than Xterminator! Contact PHILB.

MHW
Find a Man 4 Me NO LP

MHW
How Many Cats Can U Groom At ONCE???

MHW
You have the JUICE I have the IDEAS

MHW
Make the angry ghost in my apt go away cash reward $$$

With all the gravity of a man scraping mold off his last piece of bread before begrudgingly eating it, Shane calls one of the numbers. He's never gotten rid of ants before, but the creepy little assholes can't be much worse than Inferna, and will probably be less likely to retaliate.

Public transportation in Sunrise City is less than adequate at the best of times. When it's unseasonably hot and half of the city's bus lines are shut down due to the "mysterious fires" of the past several days, using it is pretty much hell on earth, or as close to it as Shane ever wants to get. Counting nickels into the bus conductor's box earns him a few dirty looks from fellow passengers, though he's never sure if it might be because of the tight pants, or possibly his hair that changes color every so often when he isn't paying too much attention to it.

He arrives at the address he'd jotted down and a man answers the door in a pair of boxers, apparently unconcerned by the fact that it's just going on four in the afternoon. "You the wizard?"

"Sure. You the guy with ants?"

The guy scratches his belly, then nods. "In the kitchen."

One step inside reminds Shane just how much he *likes* his apartment. It's clean, if a little shabby, and full of nothing but books and their few major appliances, courtesy of all his own belongings being frozen in blasted-apart ice somewhere. More importantly, it smells good, unlike the apartment he currently stands in. He also feels uncomfortably tall, shoving his hands into his pockets and unconsciously hunching, as if worried he'll smack his head on a door frame when he's just over six feet himself. Maybe everything just *feels* slouched in the apartment, he reasons.

It doesn't take long to spot the ants, mostly because there are probably thousands, maybe millions, of them swarming over every conceivable surface of the kitchen. "Wow. You weren't kidding, Philb."

"What'd you call me?"

Shane hands over the newspaper bit. "Philb?"

"They messed it up. It's Phil B. Exterminator wanted seven hundred to do the whole place."

"Maybe he wanted you to pay per ant," Shane suggests, fighting the urge to start scratching and slapping at his arms, even as his brain insists that the ants are definitely all over him.

"What'll you do it for? Gimme your estimate."

Shane squats down near one of the outlying areas of infestation, and prods a trail with just a hint of magic. If there is such a thing as extermination magic, he's never heard of it, but maybe simple energy will work just as well. He invests it with a hint of force, and that's the easy part. Briefly, he remembers how easy something like this would have been back when he'd had a boost from the Ice King. He'd remade his own hand, once, and hardly blinked at the power it had taken.

The trail of ants recoils slightly from his prod, and Shane takes that as a good sign. "Uh…" Mentally, he tallies up the utility bill and a few bucks for food. "Two hundred." He'll just hope Father Aaron doesn't skim off the collection plate or they won't make rent.

"Do I have to move out for a week?"

"You can stay on the couch for all I care."

That seems to satisfy the man, and he flops immediately down onto the couch, turning his attention back to the TV. "Go for it."

Shane raises an eyebrow. "You're gonna pay me first, Philb."

The man looks like he's about to argue, but Shane's hand is already tingling with power and that usually goes a long way towards convincing people to do as he says. Knowing he's got the cash for the bill in hand is a nice motivation, and it takes an hour, maybe two, before the kitchen is, if not spotless, at least ant-free.

Elated from his success (exterminator now sounding like an entirely viable career option), Shane doesn't even wait to get home before calling the next number on the list. Who knows how many cats he can groom at once? Probably a lot, not that he's ever tried.

On the doorstep of a woman who had introduced herself as "Barbara, I'm not a cat lady I *swear*, but everyone calls me The Cat Lady," Shane pauses for a moment. There's no cat door cut into the door.

Shane takes another look at the pamphlet, and frowns. Three of the jobs he'd circled, and seven of the Love Potions jobs all have the same phone number listed.

Before he can start wondering what that means, the house in front of him explodes into flame.

Shane slams a magical shield into place, but without being properly grounded to anything it doesn't do much except provide a nice large surface to whack into him face-first, sending him flying backwards as far as the shock wave can carry him—across the street and into an oak tree.

Pain crashes through him, radiating out from his spine in a massive forming bruise, all the breath knocked out of him without any notice. Spots pop in front of his eyes, and he tries to force his lungs to take a breath when all they're registering is pain, pressure, and *heat*.

Something starts walking out of the flames, and that's enough to kick some life into his lungs.

The shape moves fast and Shane throws himself to the side just in time, managing to register a streak of orange around something dark, his instincts telling him it's some kind of rock formation on fire. He tries to think of all the things he's fought, all the creatures he knows, but the thing is fast, cutting into his brainpower with the lash of an arm far too long to be any kind of human. It stretches when the thing punches out at him, three, four times as long as a normal arm, the fragmented rock pieces suspended in the flame as the creature moves, snapping back an instant later.

There's no time to remember past battles he's fought. Shane breathes in, the fire fueling him somehow, and makes himself a target, hoping his instincts are right.

He'd prepared himself for another punch, readied a lash of magic, but the creature turns and, *dammit*, he hadn't expected a third arm to be already forming out of the thing's torso. It shoots straight at him, hitting him in the stomach like an iron bar, searing hot and sending him flying through the air again. He twists in midair just in time to try to land, only to realize far too late that the thing had hurled him back into the burning house of Not A Cat Lady Barbara, if she was ever real.

Magical wind coils around him, sheltering, moving with each breath he takes and cushioning him from the heat of the flames. It dives into his lungs, freeing them from the smoke and letting him snarl out, "Extra limbs are cheating!" before hurling himself back out at the creature.

He takes quick stock of the area around him, and dimly wishes he still had a magical sword of inhuman ice. That, he thinks bitterly, is something like irony, that he'd lost it immediately before all these goddam fire beings had started trying to fry him for dinner.

Well, that's what magic is for.

It's easier with a real object, but a Mage of his caliber can fashion a sword like that out of pure energy itself, and he's done it before. Shane hits the ground running, ducking another lash even as his legs scream in pain from the impact, and comes up just under the thing's guard before it sucks that weird limb back in, summoning a sword of ice to protrude from his hand and skewer the creature whole.

At least, that was the plan.

A spurt of warm water splashes ineffectually out of his hand and Shane stares at it, betrayed. "That's supposed to be ice!"

The creature tilts its head under the flames, and lets out a puff of hot air.

"You can't laugh at me! You aren't allowed to possess that many limbs *and* a sense of sarcasm!" That's the rule, or at least it should be, he decides on the spot.

Muttering to himself about stupid fucking creatures who think they know a good joke when they hear one, Shane dives into a roll to get away from another lash that rips up the concrete of half the road, pulling a long curved knife out of his boot. Even a cursory attempt to coat that in magical ice fails in a sad wet way. *God fuck you motherfucking asshole piece of shit ice!*

The problem is that most of Shane's best (and in his own opinion, coolest) magic takes ages to prepare. He needs to study, to do research, to figure out how to flood objects with his power and inspire the energy currents of the world to dance at his music. Just flinging base magic around might work with ants, but it's probably not going to work with—

"Child of Flame," the creature rasps in a booming, crackling tone that almost shatters Shane's eardrums before he commands the air in front of them to thicken, "stand down. Child of Flame, follow me to The Answer."

"Asshole on Fire, not a chance." What puts out a fire besides ice and water? Shane thinks frantically, knowing he doesn't have enough juice to summon enough water to put this thing out. All he can think of is watching cooking shows and seeing chefs put out oil fires with flour, and he tries unsuccessfully to banish that idea from his mind as 'unhelpful.'

"Child of Flame—"

"You wanna tell me why you keep calling me that?" Shane demands, hoping against hope that the thing might give him a few seconds of explanation before crushing him into a burning building again.

To his surprise, the creature pauses, tilting its head to the other direction. Then it speaks again, focused so hard on him that Shane can feel the intensity of its gaze. "Offer me safe passage to your world while we speak."

"Sure. As much as I can provide." That's enough for most creatures, and Shane breathes a sigh of relief when this one nods. Safe passage, as far as he's seen in the past with the Ice King's creepier creatures, works both ways.

It's a further shock when the flames slowly die, melting back into the clay earth of the creature's body. The clay melts, then solidifies, then liquefies, running into the rough shape of a human, almost a gingerbread man before it defines itself further. After a long moment, the flames die away (or are subsumed) entirely, leaving what looks like an androgynous, clay-brown nine-foot-tall human standing in front of him, blinking opaque eyes. He steals a glance, but there are no genitals to tell him whether he's speaking to a male or female, or anything that assigns itself a sex or gender. Less helpful, but this isn't exactly a situation he'd expected to flirt his way out of, so not much lost there. "Yo. Long trip?"

"No distance at all." The voice still reverberates, and Shane becomes entirely aware that they're standing on a deserted street, next to a building on fire.

"If you want to talk, we're going to have to get out of here before the cops show up," he warns. He turns to look for a place to go, and the clay hand that lands heavy on his shoulder is unexpected.

So is the sudden rush of air and light, not giving him time to react before he's *moving*, hurtling down the street a hell of a lot faster than he thinks is really safe, especially when he's moving because something has hold of his shoulder and not a more stable and less rip-off-able part of his body. It only lasts for a second, and then he's on the ground in a heap, the clay creature standing over him impassively. "We are now several blocks away."

Shane doesn't even try to lift himself to standing. There's a fairly large chance, given how his arm feels right now, that his shoulder is dislocated, and revealing that kind of weakness to his enemy when they're essentially in the middle of some kind of firefight doesn't sound like a smart plan. Plus, whatever the clay thing is, it's a hell of a lot more willing to reason than any of the Inferna had been. "Right. So. What's a Child of Flame and why do people keep calling me that?"

"You have been summoned. Your rights have been awakened. Join those of your kind and retrieve the rest." The creature talks impassively, deep voice reverberating through the back lot of a suburb. A couple of houses away, a swing-set rocks gently back and forth in the wind. Shane still smells smoke from the fire, and can hear sirens in the distance.

"Okay," he says, more to himself than to the creature. "Who summoned me?"

"The Flame."

That brings a raise of his eyebrows. "Is it the Fire Queen? Because I was on pretty good terms with her, she doesn't need to blow up buildings or try to kill me to talk to her."

The creature turns its head to look at him. "She has no choice."

That's less good. If there's something out there threatening the Fire Queen, the very embodiment of power and rage and fire and passion that Shane's ever met, this could be bad for not just him, but the whole city. "She's targeting me, then?"

"She tries. She desires."

"Sure, sure." This isn't the first thing Shane's talked to that speaks in little better than riddles, and he's depressingly confident it won't be the last. "So, what are you?"

Opaque eyes blink, eyelids made of the same substance as the rest of its body. "I am. Clay. Impregnated by Her."

"As you do," Shane mutters under his breath. "Fine. So, can I talk to her?"

The clay thing tilts its head again, and Shane wishes he could tell for sure what the gesture means. "You still reach for ice when you feel afraid, Child of Flame. You can come before her when you fear yourself no longer."

"No," Shane argues, feeling himself get heated, "no, no, you said before you wanted to tell me the answer, you can't just go back on that now."

"I promised you no answers. I would take you to The Answer, if you would go."

Something about the way Shane can just about hear the capital letters in that sentence makes him hesitate. "Where is it?"

"Somewhere from which you cannot easily return."

It's probably bad, Shane thinks wryly, that his first thought isn't of leaving Drake behind, but of the fact that he'd *just* made enough money to pay that stupid bill for the month, and all of that would go to waste. "Is this a one-time offer, or…"

"The Answer will always be waiting for you."

"Yeah, I asked, but I didn't like that response one bit."

The creature tilts its head to the side, and Shane flaps a hand. "So, are we friends or whatever? Everything flamey that we find keeps attacking me, so…"

"You are not an easy man to contact, Child of Flame."

"And you're not going to tell me what a Child of Flame is."

"You must speak to the Flame."

"Okay, but, I'm definitely not her *child* or anything," Shane says, and for the moment, he's willing to take a lack of obvious hostility as peace. His arm is throbbing horribly, and he tries to move it back into place, only to stop when his vision goes white from the sudden pain and pressure. Right, that can probably wait for a doctor. "What was up with the phone numbers?"

"You are not an easy man to contact, Child of Flame."

That's starting to sound like a stock response. Worse, it doesn't actually *mean* anything. There's the illusion that it's an answer, and Shane is seeing it more and more as an illusion with every passing question. "If I stop trying to use ice magic, can I—hey, is this Child of Flame thing why I can't use ice magic lately?"

The clay creature only tilts its head to the other side.

"Forget I asked. So, if I stop trying to use it, can I talk to her?"

Slowly, the clay creature turns on its heel and starts to walk away.

"Hey! I'm talking to…"

"I would have taken you. Now I cannot." It moves one leg as if to run, and vanishes in a streak of brown motion down the street in the next second, leaving Shane vaguely affronted, holding his dislocated shoulder and smelling smoke from a few streets away, feeling as if he would have preferred to groom several cats at once after all.

When he finally stands, he curses at the pain under his breath, contemplates the cost of a doctor, sighs, and rests his shoulder up against a tree. He closes his eyes, uses magic to guide the bone in the right path, and slams his shoulder up against the tree, forcing it back into place.

When he wakes up, he's on the ground, fairly sure that only a few embarrassing seconds have passed. Drake has the cell phone, which is obnoxious when Shane wants to get in contact with him, but it beats paying two phone bills every month. He reaches out with his magic—something he's done a thousand times to spy on Drake, when they were separated—and tries to get a sense of what's going on. He can do a hundred, a thousand times more with a TV or even a laptop, but needs must, and Drake isn't always the best at picking up said phone anyway.

He reaches out with his presence, imagining that karate studio. It's nearly dark, and most of the students have probably gone home by now, Shane figures. Drake should be relaxed, open, his mind receptive. Shane brushes his presence gently against that familiar one.

Instead of relaxation, tension, or exhaustion, he's hit by a wave of overwhelming lust, and the sinking feeling that he's interrupting something.

The wave of emotions slams into Shane harder than the clay creature's arm, sending him staggering back against the tree. He withdraws his presence, finds an empty house, and kicks the back door in without pretense, ignoring the moral implications and flicking on the TV, a surge of will showing him what he needs to see.

Drake is stripped nearly naked. There are slight burns on parts of his body, baring his skin. He's on his back on the floor of his karate studio, hands held above his head by a too-familiar long-fingered hand.

On top of him, straddling him and grinding down against his hips, is a figure wreathed in flame.

~

Chapter Three

~

"Hey."

Drake shuts the door to the office he shares with a few other martial arts teachers, trying not to immediately let his face go sour. "You said you wouldn't follow me to work anymore."

Shane shrugs. He reaches up and brushes a strand of hair out of his eyes, a soft, nervous little smile on his lips, and Drake's anger unclenches around his chest. There's something so difficult to hate about Shane, something playful and earnest and sharp, and it hasn't been nearly long enough that they've been back together that he's forgotten how lucky he still feels for it. "Hey. Sorry I stormed out."

Shane shakes his head. "Forget about it. C'mere."

"No, Shane, I want to talk about it." Drake pushes at Shane's chest a little, but Shane isn't exactly a weak man, even if he's much smaller than Drake in a purely physical sense.

Shane, apparently, does not want to talk about it. His hands are burning hot on Drake's shoulders, pushing him back against the door, holding him there with that same anxious smile on his face before leaning in to claim his lips in a bruising kiss.

They can always talk later, Drake decides.

Far more important is feeling the heat (almost painful, Shane's circulation is something else today) of Shane's body against his, Shane's hands sliding up to pull the shirt over his head, Shane's lips and tongue tasting him, demanding him, nibbling and sucking on him.

"You can't wait until we get home?" Drake tries, feeling like he should probably make a token protest, even though most of him wants to do anything but fight against this.

Shane doesn't even speak, shaking his head as his hands slide up Drake's chest, rubbing over his nipples and making him twitch, sucking in a breath. He rolls his eyes, then says, "Have it your way, I'll just lock the—"

No sooner has he turned away to lock the door than Shane is on him, grappling him down to the floor onto his back. Shane's eyes are bright, his hands urgent, and Drake opens his mouth to protest when Shane kisses him again, tongue strangely hot in his mouth, leaning back to grind down hard against Drake's hips. The lust hits him then, hard and fast, like a mouth dragging over his cock, frightening in its intensity. If he hadn't been lying on his back, the sudden wash of need would have brought him to his knees in that moment.

"Shane," Drake chokes out against his boyfriend's mouth. "Sh—"

Shane reaches back, draws a finger down the fabric of his pants, and they erupt into flames.

In retrospect, that could have been Drake's first clue that something wasn't entirely correct.

Instead, every rush of thought he tries to have just turns into another groan, turns into his own voice whispering, "Please," turns into his hips rubbing up, dragging over Shane's ass, and when did he take his pants off, anyway? It doesn't matter, because they're here now, with Shane rocking down onto him, skin dragging painfully hot over his own, making him buck and writhe.

It takes a second for him to realize that his hands are pinned to the ground over his head. When he realizes it, he hardly cares. Anything, as long as Shane keeps undulating above him, as long as he keeps occasionally gracing him with those sinful kisses that promise so much more. Drake doesn't feel like himself, but that's fine, that's an acceptable compromise when Shane raises up onto his knees, eyes locked with his and that same smile hovering on his lips. Dimly, Drake wants to tell him to get ready, because his cock is pressed against Shane's hole and it's not nearly slick enough, but his voice doesn't work.

Then he can't remember how to talk anyway, because Shane is sinking down on him, inch by searing, agonizingly tight, inch. Shane's eyes are wild, his hands digging into Drake's chest, thighs strong and sure as he writhes down, determined and driven in a way Drake vaguely thinks is a little excessive.

Twice in their lives together, they've forgotten and Drake has entered him raw. The first time, they'd been too far gone to stop, and Shane had been deep in a submissive state of mind anyway, clawing and panting and begging to be hurt more, to be used and wrecked, and Drake had complied, finding a savagery inside himself he hadn't known he possessed. The second time, remembering how badly his cock had chafed the last time, not to mention the off-putting sight of the blood, he'd stopped, and refused to go on until Shane had done the small magic to make it easy and slick.

Both times, Drake had suspected that Shane had "forgotten" on purpose.

Now, he doesn't know. Shane is trembling and tight around his cock, and there are tears freely running down his face, but he doesn't so much as pause in his movements. If anything, he slams himself down harder, mouth falling open, drawing in ragged, urgent breaths as he rides.

Something is wrong, and Drake knows it.

Usually, Shane would be talking by now, begging *fuck me, fuck me*, craving the surrender that comes from Drake holding him down, throwing him against a wall, even backhanding him with all the power in his strong arms. Now, it seems more important to Shane to just ride him, to hold him down to the floor and take what he wants, and that's never really been Shane.

If only Drake could make himself *do* something about it, he might feel a little better about things, but as it is…

He ruts up into Shane's body, ignoring the scorching heat, ignoring the fact that Shane's had the same vaguely anxious look in his eyes since they started, ignoring everything but the wave of lust that he can't help but feel. It drives him, making him writhe under his hold, narrowing his world to Shane's ass sucking him in, Shane's pale neck exposed when his head is thrown back, Shane's hands tight on his wrists, holding him down.

It helps that Shane looks like he's enjoying the hell out of his cock, groaning softly as he rocks down, thighs working until he's bouncing, balancing with one hand on Drake's chest, the other holding his wrists to the floor. He moves faster and faster, squeezing down so hard Drake's eyes roll back into his head, and every breath he sucks in feels hotter, tries to awaken something inside of him.

Just when that disturbing thought hits him, Shane arches his back, drawn taut in sudden pleasure. That part is familiar. The part where Shane's head rolls back, he opens his mouth, and a gust of fire shoots out is… new.

Drake is probably the first person to admit that when Shane is around and his dick is hard, he's not very good at critical thinking. Still, seeing his boyfriend suddenly spitting flame is enough to wrench even him out of his stupor, still hard and buried in Shane's ass or not. "Wh-what the fuck!"

Shane groans, his head rolling forward as his back bows,

trembling and sweaty and sated. He takes a deep breath, shudders, and smiles a very different, very not-Shane smile.

Then his appearance changes, Shane's form melting away in a flash of blue-tipped orange to reveal a woman's naked body, still sitting contentedly impaled on his cock. Drake has never seen her before, but recognizes her from the description.

Her hair is a constantly changing mass of red-orange-blue-yellow, shifting and twisting and hanging far past her waist—or at least, it would if it weren't suspended somehow, swaying gently through the air. Her body itself shifts colors, sometimes pale, sometimes coal-dark, constantly renewing itself, something soft crisped to embers and born again. Her smile looks far more at home on her own face than on Shane's, but that hardly makes Drake feel any better about being under her, much less inside her.

"Hello, Drake Young," the Fire Queen says pleasantly.

Drake swallows. He's not entirely sure there's much protocol for meeting a creature whose vassals he's been killing for years, or whose husband-brother-enemy he'd helped to at least drastically inconvenience if not kill. "Um. Hello."

"I needed to burn off some of my flames before I could speak to you," she says, voice musical, filled with the occasional crackling pop. "You were most handy."

"You shape-shifted. You made me think you were—"

She laughs. "Judging by how soft you are now, I think we both know if I had come to you in my true form, you wouldn't have helped me. Are you capable, even?"

Drake's eyes narrow, and his voice is cold and hard when he says, "After what I did to the Ice King, I'm not sure you should talk to me like that."

When she laughs, she shows her teeth. They seem too sharp to be truly human, even if the rest of her belies her true nature. "You think yourself very powerful, for a man that rides on the coat tails of another, Champion. You have burned many men recently."

"I'm not the one starting fires all over the city!" He doesn't argue about the death count. Those folk had been members of the Church, most of them, and that puts them in his care.

"Oh?" She tilts her head and her hair moves independently of her body, swirling in the air.

"Do you mind getting off of me?" Drake demands, uncomfortable and more than a little creeped out by her current location, aware that he essentially just assfucked a goddess.

"I have to be quick." Her teeth shine, and she doesn't move, hand pulsing hot where it holds his wrists. "I can't waste time fighting you if you tire of my words, and you had my child remove my seed, so you will stay pinioned. There is no time—I have to warn you, before I surge again."

"Warn me of what?"

Her eyes swirl, all the color of flames that men forget about, blue-green-gold-white with heat, overlapping and melting together only to spring apart again. "You drove him from this plane. You must find him, or send me there."

"The Ice King?" Drake frowns, attempts to move his arms, and finds that she's a hell of a lot stronger than he is. "I don't know what happened to him, but I know we wrecked his place and shoved a sword into him. I'll do that to you if you want me to so bad." He probably wouldn't mind, either, not when she's still slowly burning on top of him in a way that makes him really uncomfortable.

Her fingers tighten, long nails that feel like steel digging into the flesh of his wrists. "The Champion thinks himself strong," she murmurs, sitting back and making him grunt when she sort of squashes his balls. "The Champion should think himself more humble. You want to save your city? Send me to him, or bring him back."

She leans down to his face. Every movement she makes brings that heat closer, and by the time her lips are next to his ear, his vision swims with it. "Or you will burn," she murmurs, thighs squeezing his sides. "And your lover will burn, and everything you have left will burn, and you will watch it from the grasp of my flames."

"Then give me the sword," Drake manages through gritted teeth. "I'll send you there to join him."

"That toy?" The Fire Queen shakes her head back, affronted, and Drake breathes a little easier when she leans away from his face. All the air in the studio seems hot enough to fry an egg, but at least he can get some air into his lungs before it's superheated. "It isn't with the faith-sword that you banished my King, but with a weapon of my own. Find one of his, and plunge it into my back as you did his, or find him and return him to the city." She trails a hand down his cheek, and he can feel, much to his annoyance, that part of his beard starts to crisp where she moves her hand. "Only he can satisfy my urges… but you are a good substitute, with your cool heart. I'll visit you again to sate my flames."

A wave of sudden cold sweeps through in a torrent of wind, and Drake almost cries out in relief. The frog in the pot doesn't notice heat when it slowly creeps in, but the temperature in the room now is enough to make even slight breathing a labor. He hadn't noticed the sound of the door crashing open, but the sudden rush of cold is a relief, and the Fire Queen's head snaps up. She looks injured, insulted more than anything, though her face lights up at whatever she sees. "You're—"

Whatever she'd been about to say is cut off, swallowed in a rush of force when a spell crashes into the fire surrounding her… and does nothing. Well, nothing except smashing a huge dent into one wall of Drake's studio behind her, something he notes with an internal groan. Supernatural creatures or not, they still *do* need to pay the rent.

There's some vague thought in Drake's mind that he can at least make an escape, or make a run for it while she's busy with— it must be Shane, it *has* to be Shane, who else can throw power around like that? He lurches, but it hardly makes a difference. If anything, it makes her hand on his wrists flare hotter, and he can feel his skin start to sizzle.

The Fire Queen's face sets in something like grief, and she bows her head, eyes closed. "I won't forget this," she breathes, and is gone, leaving not a trace of smoke.

The weight on Drake vanishes; not just a weight, but a *presence*, something less definable than a hundred and thirty pounds of woman, something elemental and fearsome that held him in place after he'd spent most of his life learning to fight. His arms start to throb painfully, the burns making themselves felt, and he grits his teeth when Shane helps him sit up.

No, he realizes in a second, not Shane.

The figure at his side has dark hair, but it's shorter, and he's much smaller than Shane. It takes a minute for Drake's spinning, heat-infused brain to make sense of it, making it far too long before he gasps, "Father Aaron?"

The priest gives him a small smile and gets both arms around him, helping him up to a standing position. "Glad I got here in time. She had you at something of a disadvantage, Champion."

Drake gives him a brief nod, head still spinning. "Guess you could say that." It's strange seeing Father Aaron here. He's still wearing his collar and black shirt, but underneath are a pair of very ordinary-looking blue jeans. Strangest of all, they're not in the Church, but in his karate studio. Plus Father Aaron's hands are still on him, one on a shoulder, one on his chest. It isn't as if he was *much* help getting Drake standing, as he probably weighs a good seventy-five pounds fewer, and Drake sidles away a little. "Uh… what are you doing here, Father?"

Unfortunately, Father Aaron doesn't seem to register his discomfort. He looks unnatural out of his robes, and it makes Drake want to throw a towel around him or shove him in a closet. "I came to apologize. I felt it was better to speak to you alone."

And you're always with him, he adds silently, and Drake can hear it.

"You came right in time." There's a note of suspicion in his voice. Drake knows it. That had been powerful magic that blasted the Fire Queen.

"Luck." Father Aaron pulls out a small box and hands it over. "Empty now, alas. Only good for one use. I'd hoped it would be more effective against her than it ended up."

Drake rubs his hands gently over the marks on his wrists—blistered, he notes in annoyance, before realizing belatedly that he's still hanging out of his pants. He turns to the side, face flushing as he carefully zips up. "Yeah, well, she's a tough bitch to crack." He shrugs. "Sorry about Shane. He doesn't like it when I'm in there alone much."

"Does he—" Father Aaron cuts himself off. "My apologies. It seems my virtues vanish entirely when I think of your chosen partner. I will endeavor to state my opinion less abruptly."

If he were a really loyal boyfriend, Drake thinks with some chagrin, he'd tell Father Aaron that what he wants is for the priest to keep his mouth shut on his opinions, but that's hardly charitable. It's Shane who picks the fights, more often than not, and they *are* usually in Father Aaron's house, so to speak. "I'll try to get him to wait outside more. He just doesn't approve of what the Church asks of me."

"He seems to approve of the Church's money enough when it suits him."

Drake shrugs. "We do have to eat, Father. Shane wants to be bounty hunters again, but that's a job that takes us all over." He hesitates on saying the next part, but it's far less intimidating to talk to Father Aaron here instead of in the Church. "I was close to agreeing with him. We could really use the money, and we'd be able to work together instead of separately. It's a better solution, practically speaking."

"But you did stay." Drake could do without the triumph on

Father Aaron's face. It's off-putting and makes him want to say something that will crush the little priest's dreams. "Your work is important to you. Not just for what it is, but for how it makes you feel."

If he's being entirely honest with himself, Drake isn't all that sure that he's saving more lives by being the Church's lackey than he would be hunting down the creatures of the night for pay. He knows he's a hell of a lot more broke. "Shane helps your flock too. He watches my back when I'm protecting yours."

"For our good, I'm sure."

"You told me a good thing done for a selfish reason is still a good thing," Drake counters, and Father Aaron holds up his hands in protest.

"You are fair, my Champion." It's back, the triumphant, proprietary note in his voice. "I will curb my tongue further. Are we forgiven?"

The door crashes open—that's *another* thing he'll have to pay for, because no one he knows can open a damn door in a sane way—and Shane stands livid in the doorway, magic bursting at one of his hands, the other wrapped elegantly around a long-handled knife. His eyes go first to Drake, who gives him a quick nod. Shane has a battle look in his eyes, and Drake can only imagine that he'd been spying and has seen something, some hint of the Fire Queen. Yes, the nod says. I'm fine.

Satisfied with that, Shane turns his attention to Father Aaron. "You," he snarls, and before Drake can really understand what's going on, Shane moves. He has the small priest shoved up against the far wall, knife at his throat, suspending him there with magic, as Father Aaron squeaks and tries to get away. "I've fought men like you before, I've *employed* men like you—"

"Shane! What the *fuck*, he's—"

"A shapeshifter, right?" Shane's eyes are wild, intent, predatory. "You think you can change into whatever you want and have my man? You think—"

"It wasn't him!"

"Drake, get your sword."

"I'm not—"

"*Get your fucking sword!*"

"Ch-Champion…" Father Aaron wheezes out, eyes pleading, searching.

Drake rakes a hand back through his hair, thinking fast. If he tries to pull Shane off of the priest, he might go off. Hell, he might blast him back through the wall by accident, or just because he doesn't feel like controlling himself. The sword—it's a stupid idea, but it will work, of course. "Just—just don't do anything until I get back," he orders, and takes off, running to the locker room. His sword is propped in one of the long lockers, standing on its end, and he grabs it and hurries back. He advances on the pair of them, Shane furious and tense, Father Aaron dangling there helplessly. "It's not going to work on him. It only works on creatures that aren't human, dumbass."

Shane's eyes glint. "Why do you think I wanted you to use it on him?"

Drake's teeth bare in a growl. "You *never* listen to me. My word on him should be good enough for you!"

"Why? You afraid to use it on him?"

Drake hates the challenge there. It reminds him far too much of how they'd been before Shane got his soul back, when there was no one deadlier in all of Sunrise City to mortal or myth than Shane Connell, First Vassal of the Ice King.

Now, he's merely the most powerful human Mage they've ever heard of. Drake forgets, sometimes, how truly dangerous a man his lover can be.

It's hard to forget now, when the power spilling off of Shane makes him almost waver in Drake's vision, mixed with his very human anger, holding Father Aaron a few inches off the ground. "Do it."

Drake raises the sword, and gives Father Aaron an apologetic shrug. "Sorry, Father, but this will keep him from—"

He doesn't get a chance to finish that sentence. Father Aaron twists in Shane's hold quicker than he'd ever thought possible, turning entirely upside down and landing a boot directly to Shane's chest. In less than a second, he frees himself, diving for the floor without hesitation when Shane slams his arm forward, not to hit, but to summon a blast of magic.

"No!" Drake crashes into Shane just before he lets loose, knocking his arm off target. Shane curses and bites his lip bloody, trying not to let the power out. Drake can feel it gurgle urgently just under Shane's skin, bubbling up with a vengeance and trying to find a victim. Finally, with a clench of his fist and a cry of pain, he wrestles it back into himself, collapsing onto the floor with the effort of it.

Drake turns to look for Father Aaron, but the priest is gone, no trace of him remaining but the open door of the studio. There'll be time enough to deal with him later, he supposes, and kneels down to touch Shane's arm. "Are you—"

"Get off me!"

Shane sounds more upset than Drake had expected. He draws his knees up to his chest, shivering in pain and clutching at his shoulder. "Should have seen a doctor after all," he mutters, face gone white with the strain. "Dislocated it earlier."

Drake grimaces, and his hand is softer this time when he reaches for Shane's arm. This time, Shane doesn't pull away. "Sorry. I didn't know or I wouldn't have hit you like that."

"Like, damn, try to keep it consensual. We're supposed to attack the *other* guys." Shane's voice is light, but the way it's layered over what's obviously real pain makes Drake wince.

"Who hit you? I mean, who dislocated your arm? I left you at home. I took the car."

"Your clever plans can't outwit the famous Sunrise City Metro

System," Shane says, and gives him a wan smile. "I made two hundred bucks, though."

Something suspicious must show in Drake's face, because Shane quickly adds, "I got rid of bugs, *God*, you really think I'd suck a dick for money?"

"I didn't say that."

You were thinking it comes across as loud and clear as Drake's suspicions must have. Shane looks sour and huffy, and he ignores Drake's offer of a hand to help him stand, staying curled up on the floor. It's such a strangely vulnerable position for Shane that Drake wants to play with his hair, wants to pet him a little, but there's too much tension between them to make that leap just yet. "It was a trap. The odd jobs in the paper. There's some weird thing looking for us, I don't know. There was another fire, we fought, then it just… I mean, I don't think I scared it or anything, it was a lot stronger than me."

"But you got away?"

Shane shrugs his left shoulder only, still slowly massaging the other. "More or less. I think I might have accidentally invoked some weird rite of speech. It talked to me for a while then ran away."

Drake takes a seat next to Shane on the floor. Better that than towering over him. "Then you ran over here to kick my door in?"

"Saw you fucking." Judging from the raw, tense tone of Shane's voice, this is what's been causing the pain Drake's been hearing. "You know, normally I like it when you invite me for that. I, uh, think I'm being pretty cool for letting you explain. I was gonna just wait until you said something, but… I guess I'm a lot more jealous than I thought."

Drake moves, trying to cup Shane's face, but Shane smacks his hands away, face set and angry, looking away. That's no good, and Drake moves again, ignoring the way Shane swats at him, getting his hands firmly on Shane's and squeezing them until he looks up. "Shane," he says firmly, "that wasn't anything but me thinking you were with me. She was shapeshifted into you, I didn't know she—"

The tension clears up immediately, replaced with startled mirth. "Wait. She? You fucked a woman?" Shane lets out a snort, then another. "Like… a *woman*?"

Drake drops his hands. "Shut up."

"Like an actual woman-woman? With tits and—"

"How many kinds are there?" Drake demands, face flushed and embarrassed. "Dammit, she looked like *you*, I thought you came to apologize!"

"Then you should have known it wasn't really me," Shane says, not the slightest bit chagrined, and shifts faster than he should be able to with his shoulder like that, straddling Drake's hips. "Poor baby," he murmurs, taunting and low. "Maybe I should get that bad taste out of your mouth. Think you can still handle a real man after—"

Drake shoves him down onto his back, a hand coming up to grip his throat—not hard, but *felt*, and Shane's eyes swirl dark. His posture changes immediately from defiant and teasing to open, thighs falling apart, lips parted, breath quickening.

Seeing that submission probably shouldn't make Drake as hard as it does.

He pins Shane in place with a look, getting up to shut and lock the door before grabbing a fistful of his hair, hauling him up to flip him over. He shouldn't love so much the way Shane gasps, the way he shoves back wanting more before he's had any at all, the way he lets out a low, breathy groan. "You're distracting. The worst." The sharp crack of his hand against Shane's ass makes them both twitch, him in arousal, Shane with added pain that acts on him like a drug.

Shane's head lolls forward, pressing his forehead to the floor as he gulps for breath. "We can talk about your shitty taste in priests later, I need you *in me*, shit—"

That's a somewhat sobering thought, and Drake lurches forward, covering Shane's body with his own. There's a certain element of resistance from his own parts, though he's definitely not going to say that out loud. *Damn, what I wouldn't give to be as young as he looks again.*

They might be the same chronological age, but the ten years Shane had spent bound to the Ice King had frozen his looks as well as his soul, and only one of those had come snapping back afterwards. Drake, on the other hand, feels every day of his thirty-five years sometimes, and part of that makes him remember all too well that he doesn't have a teenager's sex drive anymore. Well, he thinks ruefully, at least not a teenager's capabilities. The drive, fortunately or unfortunately, seems to have remained fairly constant.

Then again, maybe that's just because Shane is here again, writhing and wanting and whorish. He certainly hadn't been plagued by this kind of drive for the last ten years, though it hadn't exactly gone away. Maybe he's making up for lack of opportunity now.

Opportunity is all well and good, but the first stirrings in his pants aren't what he needs yet, not what Shane needs. Drake leans over his boyfriend's back, biting and sucking slowly at his neck. "Maybe I should make you wait for it."

The noise Shane lets out is nothing short of despairing. "Don't—you asshole, you know I need it—"

"Jesus, Shane, it's not drugs. You had it last night, don't you—"

Shane reaches behind to grab Drake's collar, looking back over his shoulder with a glare. "Don't you slow down on me, old man," he growls. "Not after I put up with teenage you."

That's a fair point, Drake has to admit, and he answers with another bruising suck to Shane's neck that makes him go limp. "Just letting you know what I think of you," he murmurs, trailing a hand down Shane's back, slipping it into the back of his jeans. He'd put up with teenage Shane as well, but he can't deny he'd been the one constantly, embarrassingly horny, begging for a quick suck in the high-school bathroom, taking his parents' station wagon out to the woods for a furtive hour of inexperienced humping. Shane had, to his credit, stuck around long enough for Drake to acquire some technique.

Shane arches his back, letting his knees spread apart as he presses his cheek to the floor. "You gonna tell me what a whore I am for dick?" he breathes, eyelids fluttering closed at the idea. "Even when I'm all yours again?"

"Especially." With a swift tug, Drake yanks Shane's pants down, drawing a yelp out of him. He only gets them down to mid-thigh, letting them help him restrict Shane's movements, even though he doesn't need anything but his hands for that. Shane is a strong guy, physically and especially magically, and that's part of why the sex with him is always perfect. Drake has to hold back a lot in life, even in little things like opening doors, clapping people on the shoulders, yanking on the steering wheel, so that he doesn't go too hard, doesn't hurt anyone without meaning to.

Shane can take it.

More than that, he wants it, wants to taste that power, wants the physical reminder that he's not the most powerful thing in the world, that he can surrender control and it's fine, because Drake is there to take it from him. At least, that's how Drake's always seen it.

Plus, it makes them both achingly hard, so he doesn't want to question the whole scenario all that much. "Spell," he orders, and feels the surge of magic when Shane obeys, a tiny magic that means they're never fumbling for bottles. Drake slides his hand lower, sliding into the cleft of Shane's ass, and rubs a thumb over his hole, hearing a keening whine from Shane when he does. "You're already more than ready enough, aren't you? Just takes that much?"

"For you." Shane sounds remarkably coherent for someone

whose knees are spread as wide as his stupid tight pants will allow, bare ass in the air with someone's thumb inside it. "Or do you wanna hear me say it's for anyone?"

"You don't have to say it." Drake's other hand comes up, and both thumbs slide in as he squeezes the cheeks of Shane's ass, slowly spreading him, stretching him out. Shane's fingers scrabble helplessly at the hardwood floors, and his breath is ragged. "I know how hungry you are for it. You'd do just about anything to have a cock up here, right?"

"Fuck me," Shane groans, slurred when his cheek presses to the floor.

One hand comes away, unzipping himself and pulling his cock out, giving it an annoyed few tugs to speed up the process. Fuck the Fire Queen, anyway. He shoves two fingers into Shane's ass, then a third, watching his hole clench and relax. "You're way too good at this. How many men, do you think?"

"No idea."

That should probably make Drake angrier than it makes him hard. He leans forward, stroking, spreading his fingers, stretching Shane more with every motion. "How many," he asks, catching the lobe of Shane's ear in his teeth and tugging, "when I was watching you be so good for me?"

He feels the shudder that runs through Shane's body, and his cock fills and swells. "B-before," Shane breathes, eyes closed, "I think—what, five? God, baby, that look in your eyes—"

Drake adds a fourth finger, and the sound Shane makes is almost despairing, hands clenching into fists that leave his fingers white-knuckled. "There were more," Drake says, voice low and dangerous in Shane's ear as he slowly works his fingers in and out, hard now but wanting to make this last. "I remember it, even if you don't."

"Do it again." Shane writhes, trying to get his pants down to spread his legs apart farther, just managing to get the tightest part around his knees. He nearly falls over, and probably would if it weren't for how urgent he is to shove back on those fingers in his ass, shoving into him, making him sweat, making his cock jump. "Just take me out—find some guy and ask him if he wants a piece."

The head of Drake's cock rubs against the back of Shane's thigh. It's good, but not so good he's in danger of losing another big segment of his stamina. "Do you remember?" he breathes, twisting his hand and watching Shane's eyes squeeze shut. It's more than just a rhetorical question. Towards the end of his time as the Ice King's vassal, Shane hadn't remembered much of anything about their lives together. "The first time?"

"God, *yes.*"

His name is Roland, another bounty-hunter. They hunt a rogue gang of Watersprite thugs together, and stop for a breather at a hotel bar before working up the energy to drive home. He buys each of them a drink in the hotel bar, and Drake tries not to be nervous that the bartender will see he's still a few weeks shy of his twenty-first birthday. "You…" Drake clears his throat, shifting a little closer to Shane. Shane is gorgeous. Shane is lean and slinky and knows how to throw bedroom eyes. "You know we're together, right?"

Roland's smile has sharp edges. "I have a big hotel room. Comes with a real big bed."

Drake is still nervous, and Shane takes him to the bathroom, petting his hair and kissing his face and laughing as he admits the idea is kind of hot.

An hour and six drinks later, Shane is bent over the edge of the bed, Drake in his mouth, Roland in his ass, both of them fucking him until he comes all over himself and sobs as he begs for more. The whole time, he never lets go of Drake's hand.

"Roland, right?" Shane pants, squirming back against Drake's cock, shoving onto his fingers. "Fuck, put it *in*, find some other dick to fuck me later, you know I love showing off for you."

It's better, Drake decides, if Shane *doesn't* remember everything he'd done in the Ice King's service. Sometimes he wonders if all of Shane had really survived that process. The way Shane shoves back at him, skin hot and smooth, ass pink from the slap and begging to be filled, is enough for Drake right now.

He pulls his fingers free, tracing one around the edge of that hole just to hear Shane whining for more, writhing and bucking and begging like he'll die if he doesn't have it in him soon. There's a temptation to turn him over, to hit that pretty face a few times and see the sheen of tears in his eyes, but Shane's too riled up. At that pace, he'd come before Drake even got it inside, and he still wants to enjoy the painful tight heat of Shane's body before he goes limp and boneless.

One shove, one strangled shout from Shane, and Drake is buried to the hilt, pressed up hard and throbbing against his body, dark curls nestled against the slick outer surface of his ass. Both hands come up to grab Shane by the hips, leaving finger-shaped bruises without feeling even a little bit sorry about it. "There you go, look how good you are for me," he grunts, eyes crossing slightly from the silken squeeze of Shane's ass around him and the wild, frantic motions he's making.

If Drake's hands weren't holding him up, Shane would be sprawled on the ground. Drake can feel his thighs trembling from being held together, and he laughs, slapping his ass hard enough that he hears a yelp. "Your fault for wearing such tight pants," he breathes, manhandling Shane into a better position, legs bent even farther, knees tucked up under his body as he slumps down to the floor, ass high in the air as Drake thrusts in deep and steady, riding him hard.

"Fuck me, baby, fuck me, f-fuck… more… f-f-fuck…" Each plea is weaker, but more urgent. Drake can see the tension in Shane's shoulders as he struggles to push back, to get more inside him even as he's stuffed full.

"More?" A harsh laugh, another slap, and Shane whimpers. "You can't take more. Or can you?" Drake leans down, trying to remember how to talk right when Shane is squeezing him so hard, rocking back desperate and needy with every thrust. He lets one of Shane's hips go and stills his thrusting for a minute, tracing a finger around the edge of his hole, feeling the obscene stretch and slide of his cock in and out. Shane's entire body shivers in anticipation, and Drake reaches out to grab his chin, turning his head to force the other man to meet his eyes.

It's a mistake.

Shane's face is tear-streaked and flushed, his eyes dilated and hungry, and he looks so much like *himself* that Drake forgets what he was going to say, what he was in the middle of doing.

"Don't stop," Shane begs, turning his head to close his lips around Drake's thumb, sucking it into his mouth and curling his tongue around it. He's sloppy, inaccurate, and Drake nearly loses it right then and there from how hard his cock aches. "Please, baby, please..."

Another swift crack to Shane's ass, and God, that's a satisfying sound, made even better by how Shane tightens up around him. "Yeah," Drake breathes. "I'll give you what you need."

His hips pound in a consistent rhythm, giving in to the urge to just rut hard and fast and steady because it feels great. That's enough to get Shane off, and with a particularly hard drive in deep, he hears Shane choke back a sob as he claws at the floor, feels him tighten up around him in an almighty shudder. Drake's hands tighten on Shane's hips as the other man starts to go limp, yanking him back against every punishing thrust, bruising and battering him with the force of it and cherishing the hard slap of flesh against flesh that makes them both groan.

Being with the Fire Queen was nothing like this. No one is anything like the real Shane, not the cold shell of himself Drake had known for a decade, not anyone who's ever tried to shapeshift into him, no one. Shane is pliant and strong in his grasp, trembling and pleading, softness and pleasure and determination all in one man that goes shivering and malleable when Drake yanks him close, slamming in balls-deep when he fucks the last bit of his release into him.

The first moment after sex, Drake thinks dizzily, is like waiting for the dust to settle after an explosion. At his age, and with the life he's lived, he's not entirely sure which situation he's experienced more often. This is better, though.

"For me too." The words are slurred and weak, though Drake can see a corner of Shane's mouth turn up.

"Huh? Oh." Drake collapses slowly onto Shane, face smushed against the broad plane of his back in the cooling sweat there. "Didn't realize I said that out loud."

"You can say more things." Shane tenses, as if he's about to move, then obviously thinks the better of it, boneless and exhausted, face down on the floor of the karate studio. At some point, he'd gotten his legs kicked back, still half-tangled in his pants, but at least not folded under himself. "God. Here I thought you'd be rusty."

"I literally blew you like five hours ago."

"Mmm, not that. I meant with the… the other stuff." Shane twists halfway under him, flexible little bastard, enough to look up with startlingly blue eyes behind long lashes. As a teenager, Drake had thought them far too pretty to belong to a boy, but ah, he'd been glad they had every time they'd fluttered at him when they'd taken his shitty car out to the woods. "Thought you were all goody two-shoes now. Or that you'd think I couldn't take it."

Drake rolls off with a groan, stretching out onto his back as Shane flips over to do the same. "You think too much of me. Don't lean up against me, you're too hot."

"I'm going to try to take that as a compliment."

"Take it as a statement of fact, but you're too hot to cuddle with right now, okay?" Drake hauls himself to his feet with an immense sigh of regret, stretching out and hearing bones and joints popping softly.

Shane touches his own head, then his arms and belly, frowning. "I feel like I always do."

"Yeah, well, you know you're hot to the touch."

"Huh?"

Drake frowns, grabbing his discarded jeans and stepping into them without wobbling, thanks to the balance he's picked up over years of studying martial arts. "I tell you that all the time. Did you seriously think I was just kidding or something?"

From the way Shane blinks, that's exactly what he'd thought. "But I feel like I always do. You're just cold."

Drake laughs. "Sure. Who's the one that had to magically cool down his temperature the last time he went in to the doctor?"

The laughter dies on his lips when he sees how confused Shane looks, as though he honestly can't remember. "Was that during the Ice Court?"

"No…" Drake watches him speculatively for a moment. "When you had pneumonia."

Shane's expression clears up immediately. "Yeah, I remember that. God, what were we, twenty-two? Twenty-three?"

Drake shrugs. "Somewhere around there." Every framed diploma and picture along the back wall is tilted, courtesy of how much action the studio has seen today, and he starts straightening. "You kept trying to fix it yourself, but you were too sick to figure out how to use your magic that way, so I took you to the doctor."

Shane shakes his head, annoyed and confused, and starts tugging his pants back up. "Don't remember. The stuff about being at home, yeah, but I don't think I went to the doctor."

Drake waves a hand. "Not important. It's not that interesting a story." Except it is, because Shane has a memory like a steel trap when he's himself. Despite the certainty that the man he's been holding in his arms, the man he's been bickering and paying bills with is actually Shane, that isn't the answer to all of his questions. Not anymore, not since he'd woken up on a desolate hill to find an empty shell of a man calling him *baby*.

"Strange," he says, picking the sword up from where he'd dropped it, "that Father Thomas was so scared of you."

"He's hiding something," Shane says immediately. He's still sitting, legs spread out in front of him on the ground, checking his hair in the mirror as it swirls through black, then tips itself with bright-neon green. "I thought he just wanted your ass, but maybe… I dunno, maybe he *really* wants your ass."

"And you don't think it's weird that the only time he's ever come to see me is the day the Fire Queen showed up and wanted to…"

Shane blinks slowly up at him, and lets his thighs fall slightly wider apart. "How am I supposed to know it's the first time he's ever come to see you, baby? I thought you were only sleeping around on me with God, but—"

Drake kicks his legs closed, which only gets him a laugh. "He probably just panicked."

"That sword doesn't work on humans, right?" There's an element of challenge in his voice that Drake doesn't like much. "Stuff that's still more human than it is anything else?"

"That's right."

"Prove it."

Without hesitation, Drake rolls up one sleeve and draws the sword across his arm. It bites deep, deep enough that he can feel it to the bone, cleaving his skin and flesh apart with a subtle edge that barely requires force. When he pulls it back, not a single drop of blood has spilled, and no mark is left on his arm. "Humans don't even bleed."

"That," Shane says, eyebrows raised, "is really fucking cool. I haven't seen you do it before, not when I was me."

"Let me try it on you."

The words come out of Drake's mouth before he really thinks them through, and Shane freezes in place like a frightened rabbit. He slowly draws his legs back to his chest, standing warily, eyes darting around the room as if he's looking for cover. "Drake? You got a funny look on your face."

"It doesn't hurt." Drake draws the sword across his arm again, then his hand, then his neck for good measure. "Barely even feel it."

Shane laughs nervously, tucking a strand of black hair behind his ear as the neon green fades away. The hair isn't a spell of his own creation this time, but a magical hair dye, something he'd traded some college kid with a mohawk for a week earlier that keys somehow to his moods. Slowly, as Drake watches, his tips creep into red, then orange, not that he has any idea what that means. "Have I ever told you that you get weird after sex? Because you do. The wanting to stab me thing is new, though."

"Most of the Ice King's vassals bled, eventually." Drake advances on him slowly, the sword tingling in his hand the way it does when it wants to be used. That, combined with the shellshock of watching someone else wear Shane's face and the nagging feeling he has that there's something *wrong here*, is enough to make his fingers curl firmly on the hilt of the sword. "I never tested it on you. To be honest, I never really wanted to know. I was always afraid you were too far gone."

There's a hint of anger in Shane's face now, which is more of a comfort than seeing just fear had been. The problem for Drake is that he can't entirely say *what* Shane would do, if he were really himself. It's been too long, and so much of what he thinks of as Shane is a combination of all his best memories. "Drake, stop being an asshole. You're gonna give me a complex."

"If you don't have anything to be afraid of, give me your arm."

Shane looks a hell of a lot like he's about to throw a punch. Drake sees it, and balances his weight on the balls of his feet, ready to catch the arm that throws a blow. It wouldn't be the first time they'd had an argument and wound up trying to punch the other to an understanding, but it's not exactly ideal, either.

Shane sees something in his body language and suddenly swallows hard, holding out his arm. "I… Drake. Tell me I don't have anything to be afraid of."

Drake's heart thuds in his chest. Neither of them want to say it, even if it's always been there. "It's fine," he lies, fingers clenching and unclenching on the sword as he reaches out to take Shane's hand. It's hot to the touch, and Drake can't remember a time when that wasn't true. "You couldn't be anything else."

Shane nods, face set and a little grim. "Yeah. Just don't fuck it up and switch it to the purée setting."

A corner of Drake's mouth turns up at that, and he takes a deep breath, readying the sword.

He isn't entirely prepared for Shane to tense and bolt, but he's not taken by surprise, either. Shane twists, wrenching his arm back, but Drake is stronger and holds on hard. "Shane, calm *down*, it's not gonna hurt—" Not that Shane has ever flinched from physical pain. Not that he ever would, after everything he's been through and everything he enjoys.

Shane's eyes are wide and terrified all of a sudden, and he brings a foot up to kick hard at Drake's chest, making him let out a startled "Oof" and let go of his wrist. In a flash, Shane is gone, out the door before Drake even registers him opening it.

The sword in his hand thrums, as if it's trying to tell him something.

"Shut the fuck up," he growls, and grabs his cell phone before stalking out of the karate studio, looking for his idiot boyfriend who may or may not be human.

~

Interlude

~

Shane dreams.

He's always hated that his dreams make sense, but only in dream context. He sleeps, but isn't asleep, not as far as he knows. He doesn't know these people in real life, not anymore.

Today, Melinda has a pet rabbit. It isn't terribly interested in making friends, and hides under the couch as soon as she lets it free.

"Mel, make it stop, it's chewing my headphones!"

"*You* make her stop, you're the one who leaves them out!"

"Melinda…" Ariana Connell's voice is weary. She shakes her hair out, short dark curls that bounce around her face and hide what wrinkles she doesn't bother to smooth away with magic. "You said if we let you keep her, you'd take care of her."

Shane is small, in his dreams. He's small enough to sit on Lucas's lap, but he doesn't. Boys don't do that. Lucas has homework, and works in the living room because the light is better than anywhere else. Lucas, Melinda, and Sofia are the only ones he can see, but the others are around somewhere. He can feel them.

It's warm, pleasantly so, even though there's no fire in the grate. Three or four times he sees his mother go to the window and peer out somewhat anxiously before ducking back in. "Does anyone mind if I open this?" she asks, finally, as if to give herself a reason to go back to the window.

"Is Dad late?" Shane asks. He draws his knees up to his chest, and his pajamas (plain blue, he doesn't have *pictures* or anything on them, those are for *little kids*) hang several inches above his ankles.

"He's probably stuck in the snow. He's bringing home a guest tonight."

That's why she looks so anxious, Shane thinks, pleased with himself that he's picked up on it, and sneaks a piece of gum from Luke's backpack. A guest is a lot of hard work. Melinda is sixteen years old, old enough to be helping, but she isn't.

His mother purses her lips and frowns, looking around at the room. "Does anyone mind if I open this?" she asks again, and the children shake their heads, so she raises her hands and rips a hole the size of a Winnebago in the roof. A snowdrift falls down through the hole, and she sighs, shoving the hair back from her face. "Mel, get that before Fluffernutter gets into it, would you?"

Without looking up from her homework, Melinda waves a hand, and a gentle tornado of hot air lifts the ice from the carpet and sends it sky-high, another burst of wind drying the carpet and sending the resulting water up through the hole. "Mooom, it got on my headphones! Can I get new ones?"

"Ask your father."

"I'm not talking to Dad!"

Melinda had a date last night, Shane remembers vaguely. There'd been shouting after, and Scott and Riley had let him sleep in their room.

A massive shadow passes over the house, temporarily blanketing all of them in darkness. His mother squints up, then smiles. "Oh, good. Your father's here with our company. Shane, honey, take your gum out, it's rude to make mouth-water in front of a dragon."

~

Chapter Four

~

Shane's head aches.

He finds himself in a doctor's office, not entirely sure how he'd gotten there. He remembers a taxi, and feels in his pocket for the money he'd gotten earlier—yeah, that's a smaller wad. Stupid, that was stupid, he doesn't need to be here.

Drake's words echo back to him, and sometimes he thinks he can remember going to this doctor. Sometimes he gets distracted by the click of his boots on the ground, the feel of the uncomfortable waiting-room chair, the caustic smell of the office, and the memory slips away.

Of course, he can create something out of nothing. Is creating a memory really that different? God, he should just go up to the receptionist and beg for an appointment. At least if he sees a doctor he'll know if something's wrong with him.

"Mr. Connell?" The receptionist calls, looking around the waiting room.

Shane starts in his chair. "Uh, yeah?"

"Go ahead back into the exam room, someone will be in shortly."

"I…" *I didn't even make an appointment.*

No, he had. He remembers it, almost, and wants to punch a wall. The clock says he's been here nearly an hour and, not for the first time, Shane wonders if an ant wandered in through his ear by accident, scrambling his brains and making his head pound.

The exam room is sterile and white, outfitted with crinkly paper and too many dubious-looking swabs. Shane amuses himself for a few minutes by scrambling the eye chart on the wall to spell dirty words, then unscrambles it, annoyed at his own pathetic sense of humor. It takes all his self-control not to start going through the cabinets looking for some kind of headache medicine. Well, self-control and the knowledge that doctors don't put anything patients can ingest in unattended offices.

"Mr. Connell?" The nurse that comes in is a middle-aged man, with watery eyes and bad skin, dressed in light-green scrubs. "What seems to be the—"

"Mr. Connell?" The doctor is a trim woman with her hair up in a graying bun.

Shane blinks hard, shaking his head. Can't get distracted. Can't lose focus. He digs his fingernails into his hand, only to look down and find that they're already bloody, as if he's been doing this for hours. That's so frustrating he wants to scream, and he clenches his fist so hard he hears the bones pop. His vision starts to swim, but he hangs on.

"Mr. Connell, you have a fever."

Shane shakes his head. "Always like that." He knows it, even if he can't usually remember it. He feels his attention slipping away again, and forces it back, counting in his mind to keep himself grounded. "Memory issues," he grinds out. It's easier when he talks, he finds to his relief. "I'm having memory issues, I can't—I can't remember things that I know happened, he said they happened, and it only makes *sense* that they happened, but I can't remember them."

"I'm not surprised," she says, raising her eyebrows. "You have a temperature of a hundred and six. I'm surprised you're still standing."

Shane waves a hand. "That's what it was last time. I can cool it with magic if I want."

The doctor looks down at the clipboard—Doctor Bowman, he *knows* her name, she must have introduced herself, but shit, it's slipping again—"That's right, it says here that you work as some kind of wizard? Is it possible that you could have come into contact with some kind of creature that could—"

"I've probably come into contact with every kind of creature you've ever heard of," Shane interrupts, hearing a sick pop when his thumb pops out of its joint. Okay, ow.

"Perhaps you should find a professional who's more equipped to deal with this kind of—"

"I'm not going to a damn witch doctor, I want a medical opinion."

The expression on Dr. Bowman's face is a little less than enthusiastic, and there's an amount of sympathy that Shane doesn't like seeing on there at all. "In my medical opinion?" She sucks in a breath through her teeth. "I think that having a fever that high for a prolonged period of time is a symptom of hyper-thermia. It's possible you have brain damage."

Shane's vision swims for a moment, and he suddenly finds himself fascinated by the texture of the crinkly paper on the bed—no, *no*, he's *not* going to go like that, he's *not* going to let his brain distract him. "Hypothermia," he gasps out. "What are—"

"Mr. Connell, your *hand*—"

"Symptoms!"

Dr. Bowman looks frightened now, staring at his hand as it throbs dully in his own grasp. "Um… heat cramps. Weakness, nausea, vomiting, muscle cramps, lightheadedness, rashes—"

"Got none of those."

"You look rather—"

"Headache?"

Dr. Bowman nods hesitantly. "It… can cause headaches, yes."

"You didn't say memory loss."

The doctor looks stressed out, and Shane couldn't give less of a shit. "It's… not a common result of hyperthermia, no."

Shane lets out a noise that's almost a frustrated scream. "Your medical opinion sucks! Weak! I gave you one symptom and you gave me a diagnosis that doesn't have anything to do with—"

"But your temperature is so high, you might have some super-resistant—"

"*You never thought it was important that I was so damn resistant to you?*"

His own voice echoes in his memory, loud and harsh. It shocks him into startling clarity, and the fog stops trying to take over his mind, at least for the moment.

He'd stood in the Frozen Court just a few weeks ago. He'd shouted those furious, defiant words at the Ice King, and challenged him with those words.

He'd *known*.

And back then, just a few weeks earlier, he'd believed he was showing the Ice King something, something that he would understand.

"You can't help me," he mutters, walking past the doctor and stalking out of the office, not relishing the idea of that medical bill later.

If the Ice King knows the answers, then Shane will just have to find him.

~

There was a time, Shane reflects ruefully, when he'd had a hell of a lot more juice.

It's easy to forget, most of the time, about all of the things he'd done under the Ice King's rule. Usually, he likes the forgetting. Most of the things that come back to him are less than warm and fuzzy. It had seemed like a gift, that blessed forgetful-ness. Sometimes, if he tries, he can remember—

A girl, thirteen or fourteen. Her father is valuable to the Ice King, but only without a soul. "Make him desperate," he'd said, voice echoing like the cracking of ice in their very bones. That had been a good order, just like letting them off their leashes to wreak whatever havoc they wanted, and the girl's screams had seemed so funny.

No, that hadn't been *him*, he hadn't wanted to do those things—

The Ice King decides, on a whim, that he doesn't like New York City anymore. There's someone there who challenges him. "Think you can bring the city to its knees, my vassal?" he asks, and Shane is delighted to show off his powers on a grand scale. Finally, everyone will know just how powerful he is. Drake will see, Drake will know how much he'd fucked up by letting him go. Three days later, a few confused songbirds touch down on branches in what comes to be known as the New York City Forest. No one knows how many humans slid into the ocean, or how many still live there, drinking in CO_2 and rustling in every gentle breeze.

Shane comes back to himself curled up on the sidewalk, silently weeping into shaking hands. It would be so much better, so much easier, if he couldn't remember the euphoria he'd felt whenever he'd gotten to show off. The worst part is that it doesn't feel all that different in his memory than the way he feels now whenever he does the same thing. It had been so easy to destroy an island at the wave of his hand back then. Now, he can barely shove his thumb back into joint with his magic, though maybe that's because he's getting shockingly, dangerously low on magic after the day he's had. At least he still has Drake, wonderful, loyal Drake—

"I never want to see you again." Drake's voice shakes with pain, with betrayal, and what's left of Shane's heart thinks that's hilarious. Funnier is the way Drake has been submitting references, submitting to fingerprints, and in and out of handcuffs for days, based on some obviously fake accusations Shane had made. People take these things so seriously. Anyone with half a brain could see that Drake obviously isn't a child molester, so why are they getting so worked up about everything?

It had been easier to forget how funny it had all seemed at the time. His stomach churns, and he sinks down to the ground, back against a brick wall, some bank or supermarket, he hasn't even checked.

Shane knows the Ice King can count on him. This is all he has left, now that Drake's decided to be some kind of Holy Asshole. The Ice King is the one who gives him some kind of meaning now, because there's nothing left but to obey. That's why he listens when the Ice King tells him not to kill Father Aaron. "He's not for you to kill, my vassal," the words come, crisp and fractured. "He left that path, as your family should have."

The only thing Shane hates more than a lying asshole is an asshole who tells a truth he doesn't want to hear.

If Father Aaron has half a brain, he's long gone from this hellhole of a city. Shane would be, if Drake wanted him dead. It's a damn shame, because Shane has the sinking feeling that the bastard might be a lot easier to find than the Ice King, who as far as Shane knows, is probably at least a little bit dead.

It takes a long time to pick himself up off the sidewalk. Something deep in him feels like he belongs there, on the street with the rest of the trash, watching people go by without hating themselves and wondering how they do it. At the moment, being the cocky, laughing Mage Drake had missed for a decade seems like an awful lot of work.

A minute later he feels better, and hates that too—it's just the forgetting taking over him again. Already he can only remember the horrible things he'd done if he tries hard. Otherwise, he thinks of the past and remembers a rainy afternoon with Drake watching bad soap operas, a morning finding Drake looking out the window of their apartment and remembering it was Mother's Day, a stupid fight after eighteen hours in the front of their beat-up old truck looking for a monster that might not exist, the drag of Drake's hair through his fingers both coarse and soft.

Wallowing in self-pity isn't going to get him in good with Drake again. If anything can, it'll be answers, and an end to this nonsense.

He's been lying, a little, when he says he doesn't know why he's fucking up at using ice magic. It's still there inside him; he'd just like to use magic without touching that cold core of power that he'd relied on for so long, the one he always has to keep separate from his burning center. If he wants any chance of finding the Ice King or his minions, however, he'll need to get the hell over that idea and suck it up.

The first breath is difficult on a city street, but Shane doesn't feel like moving to somewhere quieter. He breathes in slow and low, and exhales pure cold. Familiar tingling numbness creeps seductively through him, promising him power, promising him life and youth, and Shane knows the ice doesn't lie. Well, not about that much.

"Show me," he breathes, and the moisture from his breath freezes in the air, tiny ice crystals forming a heartbeat before they tinkle to the ground.

The magic tugs on him, and a wave of annoyance washes over Shane as it leads him directly into traffic. *This* is why he'd always preferred to program a GPS magically rather than use a tracking spell; at least a GPS gives directions that don't make him walk through buildings and ignore all possible obstacles.

His breath shakes as he runs, avoiding cars and pedestrians only narrowly as he follows the tug, dodging around obstacles and buildings as much as he can without losing his direction. This spell is strong, and the more he deviates the more it punishes him. One detour around a squat building gives him a splitting headache so bad his gorge rises, and only abates when he drunkenly stumbles back to the right angle, rounding the side of the brick-and-mortar problem.

"Get out of the fucking road, asshole!"

Shane doesn't even spare the shrill-voiced man a look, running at top speed as the spell gets stronger and stronger. He has no idea how far he's run but, judging from the strain on his legs and how unfamiliar this part of the city looks, he's guessing it's been quite a while. At least the forgetting isn't tugging at him. Maybe it's afraid of whatever he's going to see.

That's really not a comforting thought.

After being drawn directly to another building, Shane takes the long way around again, only to fall to his knees with the sudden strength of the pain shooting through his skull. He crawls, drags himself as far as he can in the direction he'd thought the magic was pulling him, but it only gets worse. "Fine, fine," he gasps, fumbling for the presence of mind to banish the spell. "I get it, okay?"

The spell is a hell of a lot harder to control than he remembers it being. The pain is worse than losing his hand had been—funny, how easy it is to remember that now—and by the time he manages to get rid of it completely he's lying facedown on the sidewalk next to (thankfully not in) a pool of his own vomit. The taste in his mouth is repulsive, his head aches as if someone had drilled a nail into it and thoughtfully removed the evidence afterwards, his shoulder throbs abominably, but he manages to get to a standing position. A few deep breaths, and he can think again, eyeing the building warily before circling back to the front.

It is, he realizes with a suspiciously relieved start, a pub. Weirder still, it looks like a normal pub, not one of their usual haunts from back in the day. Unless he's entirely mistaken or under the spell of whatever Mage has hacked into his brain, Shane has never been here before, and feels no connection to the place.

It's with more than a little wariness that he enters, surveying the room the way a battered, exhausted, and mentally compromised man should, he thinks—with his back to the door. Of course, that kind of thing is a lot cooler, he thinks, if people inside are expecting trouble. The people inside this establishment seem to be mainly expecting food and booze, and plenty of both. There are a few dumb college kids playing some weird version of Quarters with red plastic cups on a table, yelling "OOOHHHH" every so often. Shane surveys the scene, trying to figure out what the magic could possibly have drawn him to. The college kids? The couple making out in a corner booth across from their obviously uncomfortable friends? The bartender, looking like he's debating whether to ask for Shane's ID or not (which is flattering, but not terribly useful right now)? The two women eating alone at different booths, one obviously waiting for someone, one trying to look like she isn't?

"Dude, no fair, put that shit away!"

"I bet you can't even make it go in with that crap, dude, do it!"

Shane feels something tug at the magical fabric of the world. It's a tiny amount, barely enough to register, like feeling a droplet of water land in a lake. But it's there, and the big creatures at the bottom can sense even tiny vibrations.

Shane stopped pretending years ago that he isn't one of those eldritch monsters.

One of the college kids, a kid with the sides of his head shaved and that tousled look that is apparently so "in" right now and a T-shirt of a band that was popular when Shane was in middle school, screws up his face, staring intently at his ping-pong ball. He punches the guy next to him a little, then waves his fingers and the ball soars delicately into the air to land in one of the cups, jump out again, and land in another. It's not anything ridiculous, but it's more than the average kid his age and power level should reasonably be able to achieve.

Good enough for me, Shane thinks, and sidles up to the kid.

"Impressive," he says, and the three other guys immediately turn to him with a mix of suspicion at the presence of an adult and eagerness at the fact that he looks like he has money. Shane knows the type. The kid who'd done the magic, however, pales and drops his hand. The kraken is here, and even a tadpole like this kid can sense it. Shane can almost smell him starting to sweat. "Wanna have a drink?"

"Fag," one of the guys says in what's obviously not supposed to be a stage whisper. A year ago, Shane probably would have killed him in a way he would have found hilarious at the time. Now, he just ignores him as the other guy says, "Marshall, it's your point, you have to go again."

The kid with magic, Marshall, shifts uncomfortably on his feet. He doesn't meet Shane's eyes, and not just because he's six inches shorter. Once, he looks up as if he's about to, but chickens out at the last minute. "I'm gonna… talk to this guy real quick," he mumbles, messing up his own hair as if it's a habit. His team-mates' mouths fall open in disbelief, and he ducks his red face, obviously torn between the embarrassment of committing the grave sin of having a drink with another guy and the very real terror that just being near Shane apparently inspires.

"Smart choice," Shane assures him, and puts a hand on the kid's back, steering him to an empty booth. He holds up a couple of fingers to the bartender, mouthing, "Dark and cheap" before sliding into the booth himself. "So. You've got juice. They don't know how much."

Shane can almost hear the kid swallow hard. "It's just a party trick, man. Uh, sir."

The bartender brings over a couple of beers—yes, looks dark and smells awful, this will suit his pocket and his tastebuds—and Shane leans in over the table. "Do you know who I am?"

Marshall shakes his head, then takes a swig of the beer without grimacing. "But I know you're… yeah. I can feel that much."

Shane takes a sip and almost pulls a face, but forces it down at the last second. If a dumb kid like Marshall can do it, then he can, some stubborn streak of male pride tells him. "Your buddies don't know how much you've got. More than usual. You've had training."

Marshall's fingers tap on the side of the dark bottle, and he doesn't meet Shane's eyes. "Would you know if I lied to you?"

"That's a pretty suspicious way to start a sentence, kid."

"You're not that much older than me," Marshall mutters.

"You'd be surprised. Why, are you planning on lying?"

"Dunno."

Shane's patience isn't that great to begin with and it's wearing thin now. "Listen up. You're the one whose magic brought me here, so start talking. Who showed you the ropes?"

"M-my stuff didn't bring you anywhere," Marshall stammers, eyes wide. Shit, whatever Shane is doing, however he looks, must be enough to make this kid almost shit his pants in fear. He tries for a neutral smile, all the while aware that time until he forgets again is ticking. The headache and the rasp of ice crystals on his fingertips are proof enough of that. "I was just showing off, seriously, it's a party trick."

"That you stole from the Ice King?"

The apprehension in Marshall's face fades to utter bafflement. "The what now?"

Yeah, he doesn't have time for this. Shane reaches across the table and grabs the kid's arm, yanking it onto the table. The kid is strong for his age, some kind of athlete, but Shane is so much stronger he barely notices the struggle. The bar falls into a hushed silence, all eyes on Shane's free hand when it crackles and throws off blue sparks, and he brings it to the inside of Marshall's forearm.

"Dude! Get off him!" one of the college kids yells, and Shane ignores him, too, absently throwing up a shield to ward off the chair the moron throws at him. It breaks easily—shitty wood, he thinks distractedly, his shield is crap at best—and all of his attention is concentrated on Marshall's arm as he slowly drags his fingers down the smooth, unblemished skin, leaving shards of ice forming on the skin in his wake.

The very act leaves him sick.

It's the kind of thing he would have done before, he's pretty sure. He might not remember too much, but he knows that much. The act of turning some kid's arm to ice for his answers wouldn't have fazed him in the slightest, and that knowledge nags at him even as he stares down. The ice is white, cloudy, and inert. "It's… not you?"

There are tears streaming down Marshall's face as he struggles to pull his hand back, and even over the shouting of his friends, Shane can hear him whimpering, "I don't know what you're talking about, man, please let me go…"

"Must one levitate drinking games in public to get your attention, Mage?"

The voice is female, cool, and so pregnant with ice magic that even Shane feels a slight shiver. The woman it belongs to walks through his pathetic shield, destroying it without batting an eye, sitting down in the booth next to Shane. He recognizes her vaguely as the woman sitting alone in the corner, a tiny little thing with a smooth round face that he thinks he would have recognized if it hadn't been buried in a book.

Marshall's hand twitches weakly in his. "Shit, sorry. Here, let me just…" A pass of his hand, a last burst of his remaining magic after a rough day, and the ice retreats, melting harmlessly onto the table before Shane lets him go. The kid doesn't even wait for his friends, knocking over a table in his mad dash to get out the door.

Wearily, Shane makes a note to track the kid down and send him an "I'm Sorry" card or something, then scraps the idea as less helpful than simply leaving him alone for the rest of his life. "So," he says instead, trying to switch his cloudy focus to the potentially dangerous woman sitting far too close for his liking. "You're the one who pulled me in. Reason?"

She takes a sip of Marshall's abandoned beer and doesn't even flinch. "You're the one who tracked me. Don't you know me, Child of Flame?"

There's that name again, and Shane's heart thuds at the idea that he might figure out what the hell it means, that he might know the answers he's obviously forgotten. "You're… you were there, in the Frozen Court. More than once. Not a vassal, though."

He can almost, if he tries, remember what they'd called her. Something important. Something awesome. "You know where he is? Our old boss?"

One plucked eyebrow rises. "My task was never keeping dibs on him, Mr. Connell. Surely you remember that much." Then she frowns, looking at his face. "Or perhaps you don't. I've never seen a vassal as far gone as you that managed to return. You know what you have to do if you want to remember."

"Yeah? What's that?"

"Remember." She smiles, and Shane can hear his beer freezing over. "Everything."

"And you just happen to know exactly what I came here to ask, huh?"

She shrugs. "We aren't so different, you and I."

"People are telling me that a lot lately," Shane mutters sourly, thinking of Father Aaron and his insufferable attitude. "I'd really like to have a say in how alike me and you are."

"Why? You don't even know who I am."

"There something I can call you?"

She opens her mouth, then shuts it, eyes going wide as the door opens. Without warning, she slides down under the table, for all the world as if she's going to avoid an awkward run-in. Shane looks down, but she's gone, a blast of cold freezing his ankles. Ow.

That pain is nothing next to how it feels to be grabbed by the collar and hauled physically out of the booth by a man taller than him and twice as heavy. Drake doesn't slam him against the wall, but he isn't far from it judging by the look on his face. Instead, he produces a vial that Shane knows well, one that makes him strike out and reach for a spell—

Only to find that he's been pushing himself too hard. His reserves are dry, and he barely manages a puff of hot air before Drake crushes the spun-glass under his nose. The magic of the little artifact explodes through his sinuses no matter how hard Shane tries not to breathe in, and the darkness takes him as his body and mind go limp.

~

Chapter Five

~

It's been a long time since Drake has had a captured Mage on his hands.

Making the preparations is as good a way as any to keep his mind off of what's happening, and his own grief. This was supposed to be *over*. They've been rebuilding a life, rebuilding trust and, right now, all of that love he's held onto for the last heartbreaking decade seems like a fool's hope, nothing more.

Making the circles helps keep his mind off that. Shane will be out for a few solid hours with the entire vial of that nasty shit crushed under his nose. Drake's seen it before, back when they'd thought they could still make it work even without Shane's soul. Still, he works quickly. First, he removes Shane's clothing, leaving no extra spaces for him to wiggle out or conceal something just because of squeamishness.

Second comes the binds. Drake has a lot more experience with this kind of thing than he'd always like to admit. Though it had seemed more fun than disturbing at the time, long hours of practicing shibari and hojoujutsu on each other has *some* perks, he admits once Shane is strung up from the ceiling, ankles bound to his hamstrings. He leaves him at a forty-five degree angle, head secured in place as well, mostly so he doesn't have to lie on the ground for them to have an eye-to-eye conversation later.

This was, he has to admit, a *lot* easier when they'd tried it while Shane was conscious. This is a lot less distracting, though.

Third, Drake sucks it up, gets over his squeamishness, and sterilizes a box cutter from his toolbox. A nagging feeling tells him to use the sword but, he reasons, he's not as good at using that to make tiny, precise cuts, so that wouldn't work for this purpose. Instead, he opens a deep cut on the inside of Shane's arm, pooling the blood into a mug from the kitchen with a picture of a cat on it. It's an improvised ritual, sure, but it's going to work just fine.

After laying out a tarp beneath the bound man (they've got a safety deposit on the apartment to consider), Drake mixes the blood with the binding powder Shane had made a while ago, taken from *his* toolbox. It's mostly baking soda, but as Shane had told him years ago, it's not the base substance he uses, but the magic he puts in that makes it worth something. Hedgewitches can keep their herbs and potions; Shane relies on his own magic or nothing. That's all to the good now, since Drake is pretty sure no hedgewitch's magic could keep a Mage like Shane Connell down for more than a heartbeat.

It takes almost fifteen minutes to smear the blood and powder concoction in a wobbly circle on the tarp, and another five before Drake is one hundred percent sure there isn't a single gap or crack. He checks and re-checks the D-rings in the ceiling, checks Shane's bound limbs for any sign of blueness or excessive redness, and gets a few things ready just in case: more of Shane's sleep-dust, a lock of Shane's hair, and a photograph of them together (a copy of the original) soaked in a drop of Shane's blood and some cheap white wine from the back of the fridge, and a lighter. If things get so bad that Drake has to use it, they're going together.

The last thing he does before settling down to wait for Shane to wake up is to call the Church. There's a dedicated line for him—for any Champion, he supposes, but it's been his direct line to Father Aaron for as long as he's been working for the Church. Only to be used in a time of great emergency, it may be, but Drake can't think of many occasions that are more of an emergency than this.

"Champion? Is that you?"

Drake almost drops the phone in shock. It isn't Father Aaron's voice on the other end, but that of an old woman, throaty and content. "F-Father Alice?"

A low rumbling cough greets him, as much of an affirmative as he's ever needed. "Things are that bad, eh? She must be back."

"They said you retired." They'd *said* that Father Alice had retired. They'd *implied* that she'd been finally driven out of the Church and left to "retire" in some monastery somewhere, where she wouldn't be any more of a burden or a bother to the higher-ups inside the Church.

In the phone's background noise, a match strikes, and a second later the sound of a long drag through a cigarette filters through. "Can't keep an old dog down. If I'm getting calls at this number, she's back."

"She?"

"Fire bitch."

He'd always liked Father Alice. "Father Aaron has something to do with her, doesn't he? I was trying to reach him, but I got you instead."

"Don't sound so disappointed, Champion. No doubt you'll see him soon enough if she's making trouble." Another long drag on the cigarette. "Stop her. You won't want to. She'll cry and flutter her lashes and tell you she's just doing what her nature said. Pretty girl, turns a lot of men's heads. Half the reason I recruited a queer for this job."

"Uh."

"Don't fall for it. Don't let her get anything in you."

"Um. What exactly…"

"Fire seeds, Champion. Little orange motherfuckers. They run around inside you, calling her. Faith can stop 'em for a little while, but you've got to get one of hers to suck it out for you."

It's only too easy to remember the pain of feeling his lungs sear away, and the relief he'd felt when Father Aaron had called on… "So, you couldn't just… get God to take it out?"

"Thought you were too old for fairy tales, Champion."

Drake lets out a breath he hadn't known he was holding. "What is Father Aaron?" he asks bluntly.

"A priest."

"What else?"

"Can't tell you anything about that until he stops being a priest."

"Even if it saves my life? The lives of countless others around the city?"

"He won't stop you, Champion. He's probably curled up into a ball somewhere crying." A long, slow drag. "You want to watch out for that Ice-man of yours."

"Yeah." Drake eyes his lover, bound in more ways than one. "I figured that one out." *We're the same on the inside, you and I,* Father Aaron says to Shane in his memory. An idea occurs to him and he asks, "I know you can't tell me what Father Aaron is, but can you tell me what Shane is?"

He can almost hear her one-sided smile, leathery and ironic above the swathe of her dark robes. "Don't honestly know," she admits. "Just know that whenever she's in town, all the ones like those two start acting funny whether they want to or not, whether it goes against their nature or not. Some are working with her, but others are just… drawn. You'll see, if you haven't already. We had an outbreak of them, oh, thirty years ago, something like that."

"How many are there?"

"No idea. Not as many as there are of us, and I give thanks

for that every time I talk to God. There used to be a lot more, but…"

Shane stirs, and Drake mentally curses. "Thanks, Father. Is there… is there anything I can do about it? About them? Aside from killing them, I mean."

There's silence on the other end of the line. "Are you prepared to unmake a man, Champion?"

"I don't even know what that means."

"Rip out the core of what makes him. Change it. Put it back in dead. If you can't do that, you can't keep them alive and free of it."

Drake's heart thuds in an unsteady rhythm, and his breath comes shallow. "I'm not going to kill him. I just got him back."

"Then he'll be hers forever." Father Alice doesn't pity him. She never has, even when he showed up at the doors of the Church after Shane had gone for good, shuddering and hating himself and emotionally wrecked. She hadn't looked any younger then, and had hauled him off the ground with one aged hand, telling him, *Sisters are supposed to be comforting. Call me Father Alice.* "There are worse things than loving someone else's man. At least he doesn't belong to the Ice King. You'd be surprised, more than a few of our members went missing after he did. Covers blown, powers shattered, like calling to like. You've got to put out this fire, Champion."

She breaks off into a coughing fit, long and deep and wet, and Drake tries to keep his gorge down. "Father Alice… I have to—"

"Go. If you can man up and save him, all the better. Just don't be surprised when you find out how much of him was her all the time."

The phone clicks silent. Father Alice has never been one for goodbyes. She'd told him, once, that she'd simply used up her lifetime allotment of them long ago.

Out of the corner of his eye, Drake can see Shane start to

move, feel the bonds, then freeze. He'll be disoriented, Drake knows from experience, and then he'll try to figure out where he is before acting. They've both tried the powders and potions, to make sure they're safe and to learn how to function under the influence. "Shane. You're home."

That doesn't ease any of the tension from Shane's body. He draws in a deep breath, then exhales, eyes flicking up to Drake's in a confused swirl of colors that's deeply discomfiting. "Wasn't expecting such a warm welcome."

That's one of their code phrases, Drake remembers with a start. It's been ages since they've used them, but knowing there are shapeshifters running around, Shane's not crazy to break them out now. "Wasn't expecting you to be such a cool customer." He shakes his head. "We were really young and dumb when we came up with that one."

Shane tries for a smile and fails. "I was kind of hoping it wasn't you. Or that this could be a fun rope day. Guessing the chances of that are low?"

Drake pulls up a chair from the kitchen table, sitting a few feet outside the bloody circle. "Depends on you."

Shane takes in a shuddering breath, squeezing his eyes so tightly shut that a tear leaks out of one of them. "If half of the shit people are saying is true, you might want to leave me like this. At least it's gone in here. I'm—Drake, someone's been tampering with my brain, my memory." He gulps for air, almost panicking, as if he has to race to get it all out. "I don't know why, I don't know how long, they're just—I don't know what I'm forgetting except that it's *important*, and it's just me, it's not you."

"So you kick me in the chest and run off to get drunk? What the hell?"

"I wasn't going to get *drunk*, I went to get some dumb frat boy named Marshall to talk. I…" Shane squirms in his bindings. He looks like he's about to ask Drake to let him down, but thinks better of it. "I know I know what's going on, I just keep forgetting it. Remember in the Ice King's court? I said something about being resistant to him?"

"You said everyone was going to see why." Drake frowns and shakes his head. "I meant to ask you about that, but I guess we… got distracted."

"Or something made us forget," Shane adds eagerly, seemingly thrilled to be on the same page as Drake. "Drake, this magic is really powerful. Like, me-grade powerful. Like, I've never met another human with this kind of juice and, frankly, style."

That gets a lopsided grin out of Drake. It almost feels like they're just relaxing after a long day, minus the shibari.

All right, minus the blood circle. The shibari isn't *that* unusual for them.

"Why did you kick me, though?"

"Don't know." The nervousness is back on Shane's face, but it doesn't look like fear of him. If anything, it looks like fear of himself. "That was… some weird kind of instinct, I don't know, I don't know why I did it. Just… do the sword, baby. I wanna know once and for all." Shane's face is pale and Drake has a sinking suspicion it isn't because he's afraid of a little nick, not when he hasn't even mentioned the cut on his arm still dripping blood onto the floor.

Not entirely sure if he should trust this newfound submission, Drake picks up the sword, advancing slowly on the circle.

As if on cue, as soon as he's a couple steps away (a sword's thrust away, Drake's brain supplies unhelpfully), Shane starts thrashing as much as he can in his bonds, which is gratifyingly little. "Drake, baby, you don't have to do this, get that thing away from me," he babbles, eyes dilated huge and dark. "You know I'm human, what the hell else could I be, baby, *please*—"

"Why are you so scared?" Drake demands, stopping a half-step away from the circle, hearing Shane pant and huff and whimper. His only saving grace is that Shane hadn't attacked him magically before. It's possible, though he's not going to bet on it, that Shane will be able to show the same restraint again, and he can't exactly kick this time. "You know I'm not going to really hurt you."

Shane's eyes are clouded, uncomprehending, and wide with terror. There's little sense there, just instinctual fear that drives him. "Baby, please. Please. I'll do anything, just—don't do it, you don't want to see what's going to happen if you do—stay *back*, Champion!" His voice is shrill, ringing through their tiny apartment, and it doesn't sound all that much like Shane anymore.

Unbidden, Father Aaron's voice echoes in Drake's mind. "*If you ever need to find her, open him up. See what's inside.*"

Teeth gritted, Drake sheathes the sword. Shane relaxes, eyes returning to their normal size as he gasps for air. The sword vibrates in his hand, robbed of its prey—or its righteous slaying, whichever. "I think it's safe to say," Drake says quietly, "that it might not be in our best interests to do that."

Silently at first, Shane starts to cry. He squeezes his eyes shut, but that doesn't stop the tears, until his shoulders are shaking and he's struggling against his bonds to unsuccessfully stop Drake from looking at him. "I don't… I don't know what's wrong with me. I'm just scared, shit, nothing's ever scared me like you cutting me with that thing."

"You used to dare me to do it," Drake says, finally letting go of the hilt.

"Knew you didn't want to." Shane shakes his head and blinks open his eyes, startled. "That… was a lot easier to remember. Yeah, I remember, you used to threaten me but I knew you didn't want to. You were too scared to find out that I was too far gone with the Ice King and whatever, and you knew you'd have to kill me if you found out you were right. Shit, get closer to me, is that how it works?"

"I'm not breaking the circle."

"Don't *break* it, just come inside and bring that thing with you."

Hesitantly, well aware that Shane could kill him in a heartbeat with magic if he steps inside the bloody circle, Drake steps through. Shane, helpfully, doesn't murder him. "Hi."

"Hi. Is it working?"

Shane licks his lips, making a face as he tastes salt. "Ask me a question. Something about back then."

Drake frowns, thinking. "Why did you steal my good flannel shirt last February?"

Shane gives him a deadpan stare. "The flannel? Really? All of those years, and that's what you're still sore about?" He sighs, swaying forward slightly, then coming to rest. "I didn't, I had Roy do it. He was my bitch for a while. And I had him do it because I wanted him to wear it and shift into you when he, uh, fucked me." He grimaces. "Sorry. Yeah, it's working, though, I forgot all about that."

Drake waves a hand. It's one of the least offensive things Shane did, anyway. He hates waking up in the morning and seeing his boyfriend pale, ill, and red-eyed, knowing he'd been remembering something and trying to hide the symptoms. "It's fine. What's a Child of Flame?"

Shane licks his lips, and when he exhales, the heat washes over Drake's body. Weird. "It's..." He closes his eyes. Drake can see his hands moving, fingers wriggling as if he's grasping at literal straws, searching for something elusive. "There were three kinds of us. Oh God, this is fucking weird, baby, it's like I'm remembering all this shit I knew and just *forgot...*"

Drake doesn't hesitate before reaching out to cup Shane's face, feeling him tremble slightly. His skin is clammy even if the heat of him burns through everything, and he brushes a reassuring kiss over Shane's forehead. "You're doing great. Just tell me what you know."

Shane takes an unsteady breath, then nods as much as he can in the rig. "There were three kinds of us," he repeats slowly, like he's telling a story. "The dragons, and the goddess, and the ones that poured ourselves into human forms. The others—there are trade-offs. We got rid of most of our power."

"This is you reduced?" Drake asks, somewhat alarmed. "You're the strongest Mage I've ever heard of. What would you be if you didn't get rid of it?"

"The Fire Queen," Shane says softly, eyes lidded. "I mean, not me. I didn't make any bargain. I didn't decide anything. We came over—the dragons, they bound themselves, got rid of the magic, they put it all into physical form. Kick-ass physical form, but the only magic they have left is the fire, can't get rid of that, it's what they are. Then there's her—she's a third of the whole thing, fuck, she's *so* strong but she's nothing… nothing solid, you know? She's what she is, she's a fire, she's everything that's heat and destruction and she can't not propagate herself."

"And then there's you."

Shane swallows, and looks up into Drake's eyes. "I never knew I knew all this," he whispers, blinking away leftover tears. They hit the floor with soft pattering noises, one after the other. "It was before my time, it's when all magic came over. She's—you know how she can't help it, she's got to make more? My folks, their folks, it's why there were so many of us."

"So many?" Drake frowns. Come to think of it, he'd never asked much about Shane's family. "You just told me they all died, that something killed them. You never acted like you wanted to talk about it, so…"

"Forgot. There were ten of us, I'm the youngest. I mean, the only one, now." The emotion that flickers briefly on his face can't be called a smile. "They were friends with dragons, my folks, and they had enemies, I know they did. I—shit, I think it was the…" He swallows hard, blinking rapidly as a couple of startled tears fall to the ground. "I think it was the Church. I don't remember everything, just a man in black robes, and he—*Drake, cut me down!*"

The last part of that sounds so panicked that Drake doesn't

even hesitate. Or maybe that has to do with the way bullets come flying in through one wall, bursting in with a hail of shrapnel. They spray without any knowledge of where Drake and Shane are standing, the "spray 'n' pray" method, and Drake has no time to be grateful their attackers hadn't sprung for heat-detecting technology or a Mage. There's only the smallest moment between one magazine being emptied and the next, which says loud and clear that there are several killers outside, or one extraordinarily efficient one. Two, he thinks distantly, judging by a split-second impression of where the bullets are entering the apartment.

Drake has less than a second to make a choice, and instead of hacking at the ties binding Shane to the ceiling, he slices the one binding Shane's hands, then hits the ground, rubbing an elbow through the bloody circle. Adrenaline pumps through him, and he reaches back to get out the sword, just waiting for the order.

"Go!" Shane yells, and that's good enough for Drake. He leaps to his feet, charging at the door as bullets hit the magical barrier in front of him and stop in mid-air. That's… not ideal. Sure, it's better than being ripped apart by those same bullets, but Shane can usually make a barrier so hard that bullets *ping* harmlessly away from him instead of slowing to a stop before dropping. He casts a split-second glance back over his shoulder, and really gets it—the grayish tone of Shane's face, the wobbling hands, the red eyes, that's not just from being upset. Shane's got to be drained to the point of uselessness by now from all of the magic he's been tossing around, and he no longer has the Ice King's reserves to keep him going.

All the more reason to end this quickly, Drake thinks, and gives Shane a nod before kicking his door out. The door swings in and is not really meant to go out, but he's well over six feet tall, weighs significantly more than two hundred pounds, and has years of martial arts' experience. The door goes out when he kicks it.

Drake explodes into the hallway, only marginally confident in Shane's shield, and his heart sinks.

No.

He did *not* want to find that his attackers were two human men holding Uzi nine-millimeter guns with extended clips.

He really, especially, did not want to find that they were two human men that he knew.

The fact that both of them are wearing the robes of priests is really just the icing on every awful cake he's ever seen.

Neither Father Thomas nor Father Douglas hesitate at all. They bring up their guns and, unfortunately, ducking as soon as they point at him doesn't work; they just aim down, or stop firing. "Father, stop!" Drake shouts, turning between them wildly, sword in hand. "I'm one of you, I work for you!"

Neither of them respond to him. Drake looks up, hoping to see some hint of mind control, some kind of red glowing eyes, but behind the military-grade rifles are only the men he's known for years, the ones who'd blessed him and sent him on missions, the ones who'd answered to Father Aaron and made him feel safe and welcomed when he'd had no one.

Father Douglas has the grace to lock his jaw and look impassive. Father Thomas has the gall to look sorry about what he's doing, as if that's going to make it any better. The two of them look down at him, then at each other. As one, they move past him in what looks like formation, leaving him in the hallway as they enter the apartment.

They're not here for him.

With a low growl in his throat, Drake lunges up from the ground, impaling Father Thomas through the back with the sword. It slices through his lung, slanting up through the ribcage and through his heart, to emerge the other side…

…without a single drop of blood spilled.

Father Thomas steps quietly to the side as if he doesn't even notice, and the sword passes harmlessly through his bones and muscles together, flesh sealing after it passes through as if it belonged to a ghost. Drake curses and sheathes the sword on his back as unhelpful. Shane is still hanging in the air, hands outstretched, face green with the effort of holding up his shield, and Drake shouts, "You, you, put it on you, they're here for you!"

Immediately, he realizes that was the wrong response. Father Douglas turns his gun on Drake, while Father Thomas stays pointed unerringly at Shane, and they both cease firing, slapping a new magazine into the clip one after the other. It's Father Douglas who speaks, cold and precise. "You have no power left, Child of Flame. Let us put you down mercifully. We will spare the Champion."

"I'll *never* do anything for you if you kill him," Drake snarls, and the priest fires another bullet to make his point. It slows at the barrier, then continues through in a weak arc, thunking Drake in the shoulder with about as much effort as a thrown tennis ball.

That's *not* good.

Shane draws in an audible, ragged breath, sounding like he's on the verge of collapse. "What do you fucking want?"

Father Douglas's eyes are hard and unyielding. "Lay down your shields. It will be quick. We have no interest in causing more suffering."

The bitter irony is that the Church has only armed him to protect people against the inhuman. Drake has always been able to bargain with monsters. It's the humans that want nothing but death half the time, and are so good at achieving it.

This might look sloppy, but he can't fault their plan. Shane is exhausted, and there's no good shield from a machine gun, not in their tiny apartment. Drake has a huge disadvantage when it comes to attacking humans, and they don't have any magic that Shane could have sensed coming.

Plus, they're *priests*. Drake might not be the most religious guy in the world, but there's just something *wrong* about attacking a man in liturgical vestments, even when he's aiming a machine gun. Shane might have some memory that they'd killed his family, but Shane's memories haven't been all that reliable lately. He makes eye contact with Father Douglas, holding up his empty hands in a gesture of good faith. "Father, don't do this. We're not your enemy, we don't want to hurt anyone."

"Test the shield," Father Douglas orders. Before Drake can say anything, Father Thomas fires. The bullet slams into Shane's shield and, to Drake's horror, goes easily through as if it had encountered a layer of thick molasses instead of the impenetrable wall it usually is. It doesn't exactly go through Shane's body, but it does hit him in the belly. In his current naked state (Drake *hates* how careful he was), it's strangely easy to watch the bullet strike his flesh and bounce off, though Shane lets out a noise like he'd been punched in the gut, and a few drops of blood fall to the ground.

"Another. Aim for his eye."

"Wait!" It only takes Drake a second to pull out the photograph and lighter from his pockets. A bullet thunks into his shoulder again when he moves, and yeah, that hurts like a fracture, but it doesn't drop him. Shane whimpers from the effort of holding up the shield, and Drake holds up his prizes. "You're not aiming for my eyes," he says, talking fast and praying to a god he doesn't believe in that he's right about this. "If this catches fire, we both go up in flames."

"They were spraying this whole fucking place with bullets," Shane says, strained and in obvious agony. "I know you like to think you're special to them, but they *really* don't care whether you live or die!"

"Yeah." Drake licks dry lips, taking a final gamble. "But they might care *how* you die. I'm guessing letting you go up in flames specifically isn't going to be part of their plan." *Please let that mean more to them than it does to us.*

Suspicion narrows Father Douglas's eyes. "Give me those."

"Uh, no."

"Father Thomas—"

"If you move your hand on that trigger, I'll do it," Drake warns, holding the lighter panic-inducingly close to the photograph. "You're still not sure if his shield has faded enough, right? You might not be able to kill him with that bullet, but I sure as hell will, and then it's… well. You guys know better than me what's going to happen then." *Hopefully, because I have no idea.*

Father Douglas shrugs minutely. "Then we'll simply wait. He's fading so quickly, it won't take us long to be sure."

Damn. Drake's hope freezes and his thumb wavers on the catch of the lighter. "He's not a battery. He can hold out longer than you think."

At least, he really hopes Shane can. He's never seen the Mage fade so quickly, no matter how tired they were, unless he was trying to work several spells at once.

A thought catches and he tries to keep from letting his eyes flick immediately to Shane, for fear that he'll give something away, or at worst, see that he's wrong. Is he wrong? Is Shane just overwhelmed? Has he lost too much blood?

Blood.

He hadn't needed too much for his temporary rig on Shane, because blood is one of the most powerful magical substances there is. Mixing it with the binding agent is a great way to bind him, sure, but it also keeps it from being *pure*. Pure blood, a Mage's blood, is the most potent ingredient Shane could ever have to work with, his own even more.

And there just happens to be a pool of it that's been forming underneath him for several minutes.

Drake watches Father Douglas waver and resolutely keeps his eyes up and away from the pool of blood on the ground. He wants to ask, to find out if he's just crazy or if he's crazy right, but…

If there's ever a time he's needed to trust Shane with his entire life, it's now. Honestly, it isn't that hard a decision. "Suppose we don't get a chance for last rites?" Drake tries lamely, on the offchance that Shane might need an extra minute. "Seems rude after all I've done for you."

"Sorry, Champion." Father Doulgas's gun doesn't waver. It isn't the best gun in the world, but with as many shots as the magazine can hold, it's one of the most lethal at close range. "I'll say them afterwards and lay you to rest."

Shane isn't cracking jokes. That should be cause for alarm, but Drake knows better. The only time Shane doesn't crack jokes, especially with such ripe material, is when he's concentrating. Usually murderous priests saying things like *lay you to rest* would have been prime material.

Father Douglas loses his patience. "Try his shield again," he orders.

Father Thomas doesn't obey.

Drake steals a look, but Father Thomas is frozen in the same spot he'd been in, gun aimed right at Shane. Slowly, he reaches down to the ground and drags his hand through the pool of blood under Shane's forearm.

"Thomas!" Father Douglas swings his gun around to point it at Shane and pulls the trigger. The trigger clicks back, but no bullet speeds out. Shane's face is contorted in concentration, eyes shut as Father Thomas suddenly lunges forward, smearing a long red trail down Father Douglas's face.

Slowly, Father Douglas sets his gun down. His hand hesitates on the trigger, as if an internal war is going on inside of him, before finally straightening up. Now, Drake can see it—a thin trail of blood snaking its way up Father Thomas's boot to wrap around his leg. Skin-to-skin contact is important, and for Shane to summon up the mental energy to move his blood at the same time as formulating some kind of mind control *and* holding up some semblance of two shields...

Drake can see why everyone is afraid of his boyfriend, sometimes.

"Are you going to kill them?" he asks, watching the two priests stand perfectly still next to each other.

Shane's breath is a weak little wheeze now, and he sags down against the ropes. The in-the-moment magic is done, and Drake knows what kind of drain shielding especially puts on him. Shane is great at slinging death around and plotting out intricate spells to go with technology, but defensive magic is something he's never been too good at. "Dunno what else to do. Yeah. No," he says suddenly, frowning. "It wouldn't make a difference. If they don't show up and we're still alive, they'll know what happened. If they go back and we're still alive, same thing."

"You… you don't want to…"

Shane doesn't even have the energy for a sad smile. "The fact that you still assume I'd want to hurt them, or whatever, really doesn't make me feel great, baby."

"The fact that you took so long to stop them didn't exactly do wonders for me," Drake grumbles, sitting back against the wall and hearing his bones creak in protest.

"If I just wanted to stop them from shooting," Shane says, "I'd have just stopped up the firing mechanisms of their guns. Duh."

Come to think of it, Drake *has* seen Shane do that before, lots of times. "Why the hell didn't you?"

"Didn't know what they wanted. Didn't know what they were planning." Shane bites his lip, worrying at the chapped skin until it bleeds slightly. "I thought if they knew they couldn't kill us with those, they'd pull out grenades or some shit, I don't know how nutty your religion is or if these guys are ready to die to bring me in."

Drake hears that like a blow. "I didn't even think of that." The more he thinks, now that his pulse isn't racing from adrenaline, the more uncomfortable he is. "I mean, I guess it's safe to say they're not too invested in keeping me safe anymore. Shane they're *everywhere*. If the church decides to come after us…"

"I know. We'd be better off running than fighting." Shane slumps against the ropes, less in relaxation and more in shivering exhaustion. "Drake… you've got to help me out. I've got nothing left."

Drake rubs his forehead, eyeing the two priests still standing stock-still. Being vulnerable at a time like this isn't exactly something he craves, especially not when he knows there's probably going to be worse still to come. Their lives do tend to work out like that. "Want me to cut you down?"

Shane shifts experimentally, then shakes his head. "It's surprisingly comfortable, and it keeps me from moving accidentally and wasting energy."

Drake grimaces. "That bad, huh?"

"Been better. Come kiss me, I'm gonna suck out your life force."

Drake levels him with a look that isn't anywhere close to amused. "That was a lot cuter before someone yanked your soul out, you know."

"Nah, I'm always cute." Shane might be speaking more normally, but there's still little life in his voice.

Drake steps forward, cupping Shane's face in his hands. Even at just that touch, he can feel some of his vitality, some of his strength for the moment, bleeding away, as if he's a puddle of water too close to a bone-dry sponge. He'd only seen Shane like this twice before. Once had been in their teenage years, when they'd followed a Darkfae into a trap and Shane had nearly destroyed half of a very important geological site trying to get them out alive. That odd draining sensation had been new then, and Drake had been almost positive that Shane wouldn't be able to stop, that he'd wind up dying that way, and he'd struggled against his fate. The second time had been three years ago. Shane had been drained to the point of death in some fight against the

Ice King's enemies, and had showed up on Drake's doorstep like that. At the time, he'd thought it would be better, more humane, just to let him die.

"You let me in anyway."

Shane's hands are the only things he can move, and he brings them up to Drake's face, carding his fingers gently through sweat-damp hair. They're as cold as Drake's ever felt them without ice magic being at play, and startlingly weak when they reach to pull him closer. "I remember that much." The tone of his voice says that it's not an entirely happy experience. "You're still wearing the sword."

The lines of stress on Shane's face are long enough. Drake doesn't want anything adding to them. Besides, the sword isn't much help to him against priests with machine guns, apparently, so there's little real choice involved. He unstraps the sword, laying it down a few paces away, and shoots an apprehensive glance at Father Thomas and Father Douglas. "They're... not gonna wake up while we're doing this, are they?"

"Nah. Probably not." Shane's face is gray enough that right now he doesn't even care all that much.

Touch is all Shane needs to absorb some of that life essence, some of the energy, which most humans just waste anyway. The problem is, the more they touch when he's like this, the more it charges him up, the more he needs more, the more he's desperate for that touch. Drake had tried to give it to him without sex before. Right now, he's not sure he can handle seeing Shane furious, crying, and begging all at once, not when he means it.

He steps forward and trails a fingertip up Shane's naked back. Shane wriggles, whimpering at the contact, and even that much makes Drake feel a little lightheaded from the way Shane just sucks him in. This is a dangerous game, he knows. He'd trusted Shane the first time because he hadn't known what the process entailed. He'd agreed the second time because right then, with

Shane on the brink of death, Drake hadn't cared too much if he lived to see the next lonely day.

I guess I do still trust him, after all.

Before letting Shane down, Drake teases him for a minute. The more he can feed Shane little bits and bursts of power, the less he'll be frantic when they can have full-body contact. He rakes his nails lightly down Shane's torso, then leaves a long sucking bite to one muscular shoulder. With every touch, color returns to Shane's skin, radiating out from the point of contact. "I could mark you up like this," he whispers, and gently rubs his thumb over the head of Shane's cock, dragging a gurgle out of him. "I'm bringing you back to life a little at a time."

"Might as well." The words are a little wet, a little helpless. "You're the only reason I'm here."

That's enough teasing. Drake moves, taking some of the weight of Shane's body in his hands, giving his limbs some long-awaited relief from the press of the ropes, and Shane gasps. Of course, that might have less to do with the start of circulation, and more to do with the way Drake feels energy rushing out of him into Shane.

"S-sorry," Shane whimpers, clinging weakly to him as Drake lifts him from the ropes, sliding loops over ankles and between thighs. "Sorry, I can't do anything about it, I'm not doing it on purpose."

"I know. It's fine." Drake lowers them both to the ground, trying to keep as much contact as he can, soothing Shane with his lips, his hands, the press of his body strong and sure against Shane's.

It's been long enough that he'd forgotten the way Shane flips him onto his back, hands aggressively roaming when he crawls shakily on top. "Keep your hands to yourself," he advises, and grabs some of the rope to start looping it around Drake's wrists. "I've got to control this, and you're grabby. Got to make sure I—nn—don't lose it and suck you dry."

"You won't."

Shane's chin quivers slightly. He's got to be beyond tired if he's letting himself show that much emotion so easily. Even his lips are cool to the touch when he gently presses them to Drake's forehead, then his mouth. "Your trust means so much to me after all this, baby. I'm—I'll make it good, I swear."

The rope is good quality, but there's still a bite to the fibers. Drake flexes experimentally, determining that he could definitely get out if he needs to, and relaxes, satisfied. It's to remind him, more than anything, and Shane will take care of him. Shane always does, if he can.

If.

Shane's magic recharges automatically, over time. Shane would say that it doesn't *recharge*, it regrows, like clipped fingernails or hair, but more like a houseplant that his very existence depends on (a metaphor Drake isn't sure is accurate, but Shane always got better grades, even if he didn't go to class as often). Just because there's nothing they can do to make it grow instantly doesn't mean that a good rain and a good mulching won't help, and Shane is grinding on him like his dick contains the sunshine he needs to photosynthesize.

Maybe Shane isn't the only one making weird metaphors.

Drake doesn't know how it works, and he doesn't know why it works, and he honestly doesn't care as long as it works. If Shane can gyrate on top of him for a few minutes and feel less like death warmed over, so much the better.

Shane sits back on his heels, the color still drained from his face. "You've got to work with me," he complains, stripping Drake's pants down and off of his legs, apparently unconcerned with the priests still standing motionlessly by. "I've got to—I need more today. I hope you don't mind too much."

The first cool touch between Drake's legs makes him suck in a breath. He doesn't bottom often, and having done so just a couple weeks prior, it feels like way too soon for it to be an itch he needs scratched. Still, if it'll make Shane feel better, he'll do pretty much anything, and he's not entirely sure he can get it up again after fucking twice earlier today. "Yeah, just do it."

Sudden heat flares in the room, so hot and so bright Drake flinches and his eyes squeeze tightly shut. Even behind his eyelids, he can see the white-range flare. Before he can open them again, a silken woman's voice purrs, "Yes, Child of my Flame. Just do it."

~

Interlude

~

Shane remembers, sometimes, but only in his dreams. Magic had been so easy when he was a child, born with power in one hand and control in the other. He remembers things he's not sure he should, things that happened too young for any real memory to exist—his sister dangling loose toys over his crib and laughing in delight when he made them rotate, whizz around the room. "Daaaad!" Sixteen-year-old Melinda had called, forgetting to snatch up the toys before they toppled all around her infant brother. "The new one is good, he can stay in my room."

Melinda's hand hadn't felt cold to the touch. It was only later, much later, that Shane had learned that everyone outside of the family is cold inside.

Once, he remembers meeting a normal human. She'd gotten lost, wandered onto their property by mistake. She'd been around Shane's age, but his mother wouldn't let him speak to her. "She doesn't know an awful lot of things," she'd explained gently, as Liam had entertained the girl with some kind of clapping game until her parents could be reached. "If you tell her, she'll only be confused and call you a liar."

Most of the time, Shane dreams of his first day in foster care.

The Cooper family has never taken in a foster child before. Shane moves his things into a room painted bright pink with yellow ducks on the wall. If he looks closely, he can see the dust pattern on the wall from where a crib had obviously stood for years. "We can paint it, if it looks like this is going to work out," Mrs. Cooper says, wringing her hands slightly.

Shane doesn't know what to say. He still remembers seeing his family—

No, he doesn't.

Seeing his mother—

No, it was a gun, his father had shot them all.

And a man in black robes, calling someone "soft-hearted" for wanting to spare the youngest, calling him "an abomination"—

His head aches, but that's from the bullet. A bullet had grazed his head. The doctors he doesn't remember had been very good, probably, because he doesn't even have a scar.

He doesn't even have a mark, but there must have been a bullet, because his head aches abominably all the time, especially when he thinks of his family.

Shane's head throbs every time he tries to talk to the Cooper family. After a few months, a priest in black robes comes in a very nice car to take him to another foster home. Mrs. Cooper cries, but she'd never repainted the pink room, either.

~

Chapter Six

~

It takes all of Shane's control to stop moving. Even then, he aches with the need to move, to take from Drake some semblance of life, to claw his way back from the chill of death he feels trying to suck him in. He knows what his limits are very well, and had consciously gone far beyond them, leaving himself a pale and shivering husk.

But if the Fire Queen wants him to fuck his boyfriend, there's almost nothing he wants to do less. His stubborn streak isn't his proudest quality, but he can't really deny it either.

"How about," he pants out, fists balled on Drake's chest, "you get the hell out of my apartment? I'm not your kid, stop calling me that."

Searing heat caresses his face, but doesn't burn. Shane is probably strange for finding it somewhat comforting, but it feels like… home, somehow, when the Fire Queen touches his cheek. "You are from my flame. I shared it, with those like you, and with those like my other children. I burn." Her last words are urgent, needy, and her hands come to rest on his shoulders from behind.

"Take the Champion," she whispers in his ear, coming to press up behind him. "Burn the flame off for me and take the magic into yourself."

"I don't know what all you know about me," Shane mutters, trying as hard as he can not to take anything from Drake at all, terrified the Fire Queen will somehow use it against him even as his vision goes gray around the edges, "but I don't do real well with orders. Or threats. Or women who want to bone me, seriously, I can feel your tits against my back and it's weird."

She shifts, and the breasts are, disconcertingly, gone. Instead, the smooth flat plane of a man's torso presses against his back, accompanied by an answering hard length against his ass. "Better?" She purrs, in a decidedly masculine tone.

"I'm not gonna say it's *worse*," Shane allows weakly, and looks down at Drake.

Drake swallows. "How much time do you have?"

Shane knows what he means without asking—before the vacuum, before the dangerous lack of life force makes him collapse in on himself. Spots are already appearing in his vision, and he knows Drake can feel him shaking. "Until I lose consciousness? A couple minutes."

Drake yanks hard and his hands come out of the binding, moving to squeeze Shane's. "Just do it," he says softly. "We'll deal with the rest of it later. I don't mind."

"Not your sexiest invitation," Shane grunts, but he can't stop himself anymore, not even to stop the Fire Queen from burning off or whatever. He wraps a hand around Drake's cock, unfortunately soft by now, but that's never stopped him before. "If you want, I can ride you." Drake gets vulnerable when he bottoms and, to Shane's knowledge, never has when anyone else has been involved.

Drake shakes his head. "You need to do it now, it'll take me a while. Just do it." He softens the words with a half-smile and drops his voice. "I want you in me."

Shane lurches up to claim his mouth in a hard kiss. Drake tries to grab at him, but Shane grabs his wrists and holds them down. "Can't just grab at me right now, baby," he gasps, trying to ignore the heat behind him wriggling in pleasure. "I'll take too much, just let me—yeah, just let me in."

He *likes* to be gentle with Drake. It's glorious, taking him slowly and watching him open up, sliding his fingers in first and watching his face change from discomfort to reluctant pleasure. Sometimes he'll use his tongue instead of his fingers, knowing how much Drake starts getting vocal when he does that.

There's no time. He needs *more*, needs the heat of Drake's skin on his, needs the brutal slide of *claiming* if he's going to live through until tomorrow. Without thinking, he mutters the spell to make himself nice and slick.

It nearly kills him.

For a second, all Shane can hear is a roaring in his ears, and then there are hot strong arms supporting him, cradling him like a mother's newborn son. "Careful," the Fire Queen whispers. "Careful. I can't lose you, too."

Shane is about two breaths away from simply lying down and waiting for death. Then Drake lets his thighs fall apart, and suddenly life seems worth living again. *Priorities*. Shane crawls up between his legs, limbs inaccurate and clumsy, and he buries his face in Drake's broad, strong chest as he shoves inside.

The rush of power into him, the rush of *life*, is nothing he's ever felt before in this magnitude. The black hole inside him sucks all of that power in, the power Drake doesn't know he has. Life energy, simple in most humans, grown wild and indomitable in a man like Drake, is enough to bring Shane back from the brink of death. He feels it bleed into him with every thrust up inside Drake's ass, drinking it hungrily when Drake gasps and clings to him, riding out the sensations.

"Fuck me," he hears, the words falling quietly from Drake's

lips as his eyes slide shut. Even when he's not feeling the itch, apparently, he can enjoy himself.

Shane doesn't even have the energy for a witty comeback. His body moves, tongue dragging over a nipple and making Drake squirm, thighs flexing as he slides in, stretching Drake out without any preparation, stuffing him slowly, inevitably full. "You look so good. Fuck, baby, you look so good on my dick."

Apparently, judging by the way Drake shivers and his head tips back, that's the right thing to say. Shane laughs, bending his head to suck and nibble at Drake's collarbone, leaving a trail of red swollen bites behind. "You're such a damn sucker for flattery. Makes me want to fuck you harder."

"Do it."

The way Drake arches his hips leaves little to the imagination. He's getting hard, and his cock rubs slick and wet against Shane's stomach as muscular arms flex, trying not to pull Shane down faster. Drake still has his eyes squeezed shut, maybe because he's enjoying it so much, probably because it makes it easier not to look at the blazing presence behind Shane.

As if the thought summons her, Shane hears a voice saying breathy into his ear, "You draw me in, Child of Flame."

Before he can say anything to that, Shane lets out a startled shout as a thick presence starts working into his ass, spreading him wide without any preparation. He goes abruptly still, buried in Drake, sweat beading at his hairline as he gulps for air at the sudden startling intrusion. "I—stop, get *out*—"

Someday, Shane's reflex to draw on magic for every problem is going to get him killed. He reaches for it automatically now, scraping the bottom of his dangerously low reserves, and stops, swaying in place. Not from the amount of power he has left—he can borrow that from Drake when they're joined like this, creating this—but at the feeling of the Fire Queen inside his head. Drawing on his magic lets him feel the Other, the Ether, that plane of being that he only vaguely understands. It lets him sense energies, lets him sense magic users, and at the feeling of the Fire Queen the sweat on his brow goes cold.

"I need to burn it off," she whispers, and shit, yes, she *does*. If he's on empty, she's as far past full as she could possibly be. For the first time, Shane truly understands why there are fires being set all over the city. If he'd been holding as much contained energy as she is right now, he'd probably have exploded, and not like a Monty Python character—more like Mount St. Helens. That's the magnitude of the energy he feels in the being that feels like warm skin and bends over his back, fucking him in time with his thrusts.

Shane grabs Drake's face, urging, "Open your eyes, baby. You wanted to share me, right?" Even saying the words brings him back to full hardness inside Drake, and he feels his boyfriend arch.

Drake opens his eyes. Shane has no idea what the man behind him looks like right now, which probably shouldn't be that much of a turn-on. Muscles in his arms and shoulders flex as he leans forward, tipping his weight so he can thrust in hard, clenching down on the cock inside him. "We've never done this before," he pants, mouth sloppy on Drake's neck. "Mm, you taste so good, fuck, you like watching me get fucked?"

Drake nods. It's obviously a struggle for him not to yank Shane down where he wants him, but he's being good, at least for now. "You make the best faces," he admits, voice husky and low. He licks his lips, chest heaving with every thrust. "I like seeing you take dick. Especially mine."

The words sear into Shane's mind, and he ruts forward helplessly, driving into the slick tight heat of Drake's body. Being filled at the same time is overwhelming, and for a second he almost forgets about Drake, rocking back onto that thick cock inside of him, stuffing him full in all the right places, making him stretch and writhe around the insistent press.

Drake's slap brings him back to Earth. "Focus," he growls. "Don't get lost on someone else's cock."

"Can't help it." The energy he's getting from the Fire Queen is better, more *potent* than anything he's ever siphoned off of Drake. "F-fuck, it's good, baby…"

"Tell me." Drake's voice is commanding, controlling. "Tell me how that feels in you."

Shane bites his lip, feeling an old cut reopen as he rocks. "Like I'm gonna split open, fuck, it's so much, baby, I'm so full, you know I love dick."

"Yeah? Not just mine?" Drake's eyes are intense, but Shane can see the love there. Every time Shane moves against him, inside him, he can feel himself coming back to life. Every time that hard thick cock spreads him open, Shane can feel himself squirming in pleasure. He can't help himself, grinding down in search of that perfect feeling, something slightly elusive.

Then it presses up inside of him just right, and Shane's mouth falls open as he starts panting, shoving himself back without a care.

"Whore," Drake accuses breathlessly, even as Shane can feel Drake's cock leaking against his belly. "Once someone's got you like that you can't even think, can you? You just need more."

"More," Shane agrees, mindless and lost in a wave of pleasure. His thighs tremble as he forces himself back, forces it farther inside him even as the stretch of it makes him ache.

"Yeah? What do you think he looks like?" Drake brings a hand up to caress Shane's face gently, even though Shane had warned him to be careful. This is as careful as Drake ever is during sex. "Who do you think is fucking you, filthy slut? Do you even care as long as he's got a big dick?"

At the moment, that *does* seem like the only important thing. The combination of being fucked hard and feeling life flow into him is more than heady, it's intoxicating. Shane has never felt so high, so grounded in his body at the same time, lost in ecstasy. He only catches a few words Drake is saying, enough to make his cock harder. "Just fuck me," he begs, world narrowing to the tight squeeze of Drake's ass and the huge cock taking him from behind. "Please, *please* fuck me…"

The hands that grab his hips feel familiar, as familiar as Drake's, when they yank him back, forcing that cock so far inside him he yelps. They aren't Drake's hands, though—those are sliding up his belly, rubbing over his chest, pinching and squeezing his nipples until he's whining at the pain that spikes through him, even if it just makes everything darker and more delicious.

The whole time, he can't get over the feeling that he's riding a whirlwind, getting fucked by a tidal wave, giving himself up to something so much bigger than himself he can't even begin to comprehend it. In the moment, as far gone as he is, he doesn't even mind.

"Let the Champion go, Child of Flame."

The voice in his ear is rough and masculine, but still laced with smoke. It takes long seconds for the words to make sense to Shane in his current state, until he looks down and sees Drake. His complexion is ashen, his hands cool to the touch, and Shane only vaguely notices the splash of white on his belly. He slides out, cock still achingly hard, and Drake gives him a wry grin. "You're going to have to finish him off," he says to whoever's fucking Shane, sitting up on his elbows. "I want to watch."

Shane doesn't even have time to apologize for not being careful. The Fire Queen puts a hand between his shoulderblades, shoving his chest down to the floor and hiking his ass up into the air. In that position, that cock can take him harder and deeper, filling him to the brim so much that Shane starts to cramp. He lets out a low, keening groan, nails clawing at the hardwood floors for some relief, but every thrust is harder and harder.

His world narrows to the slap of flesh on flesh, no doubt reddening and bruising his ass with every thrust. His skin tingles with the energy flowing into him, even if part of him is slightly horrified on an intellectual level about what's happening.

"If it's just touch you need," Drake says in that sleepy, half-aroused way he gets when he's thoroughly satisfied, "I should let her bring in her friends. How many could you take at once, do you think?"

"So many." The words come out even though Shane had intended to say, *No more, please, it's enough.* Maybe his subconscious is an even bigger slut than he'd thought, he thinks ruefully, mouth parting at the rough treatment.

Drake looks up, eyes challenging as they meet the Fire Queen's gaze. "Can you make more? Like you? Or bring your vassals, I don't care. Give him what he needs."

There's a brief moment of panic for Shane. They'd talked about this sort of thing, even gone to a magical orgy once or twice, but they'd never gone *this* far. The idea is hot, sure, but it's also a little terrifying. He's not sure how many of the Fire Queen's vassals he'd honestly want having him, much less—

The Fire Queen chuckles. She, obnoxiously, doesn't sound like this is any sort of abnormal activity at all, nor does she sound in the slightest bit as if sex this rough has taken anything out of her. "Is this what you want, Champion?" she asks, and the room fills with men.

More specifically, the room fills with *Drake.*

Drake grabs Shane's chin, eyes bright when his cock slides past Shane's lips. The taste is wrong—he could give the false Drake lessons on the taste, namely that it shouldn't taste that much like ash, but the idea of sucking Drake while being fucked is *always* a good one. Some of them are even wearing denim just opened at the crotch. How the Fire Queen knows about that particular fetish of his, Shane has no idea, but he's not going to look a gift horse in the mouth just yet.

Someone grabs his hair—Drake. Drake grabs his hair, shoving his head down farther on that familiar cock, and Shane shudders. It's too much, he's too wound-up, and the next time the man in his ass drives in, he comes hard, spilling over his belly a little more with every thrust, hearing it drip onto the ground in a steady stream.

God, it's been forever since he's had an orgasm without touching his own cock at all, and the sensation is stranger and more intense than he'd remembered. It takes a long time for him to stop shaking, especially when Drake is pinching and biting at his nipples, when Drake is grabbing his hand and forcing it to his cock, when Drake is coming on his face and telling him to lick it all up like the good boy he is.

By the time Shane starts to breathe normally again, the color is back in the real Drake's cheeks. He looks more alive, more human than Shane was expecting, and that's a hell of a relief. What's less of a relief is how brightly Drake's eyes are gleaming. "You don't have to stop." His eyes are locked on Shane, but he's not talking to Shane. "He can take it."

"Drake…"

Drake grins. He reaches a hand down, slowly palming his cock as he takes in Shane's spit-glossy lips, his hole stretched wide, the bruises all over his skin. "You were the one teasing me about my stamina. Who's the one wimping out now?"

Shane wants to say that it's not *fair*, but the way he still feels too weak to push any of the Drakes away speaks more for why Drake is doing this than any sexual perversion. Okay, maybe *some* sexual perversion. There's certainly a light in Drake's eyes that he hasn't seen on too many occasions. "Drake," he tries, but then there's a cock down his throat and strong, callused hands on his cheeks, and he doesn't get to talk anymore.

The next few hours are a blur of hands and tongues and cocks. Shane thinks the real Drake joins in sometimes, but damned if he's not entirely sure. Someone is always fucking him, hard and deliberate, setting a rhythm he feels in his very bones.

When he's nice and loose and spasming with his ninth orgasm, the one behind him laughs and lifts him. He barely has time to mumble anything about being at his limit when a second cock joins the first one, stretching him impossibly wide. He screams around the hard flesh in his mouth, but no one listens, holding him down and using his body in ways he's only seen on Japanese porn sites. There's a vague memory of something like this in the Frozen Court, but Shane shoves that thought away. There's no magic keeping him from remembering it—his mind has rarely felt so clear of magic—but it's nothing he wants to think about when he's enjoying himself so utterly.

An indeterminate number of hands squeeze him, and sometimes slap his ass, backhand him across the face when he writhes in pleasure at a particularly hard thrust. It might be Drake. It might be someone else, some strange Fire clone that only looks and acts like Drake. Shane doesn't know, and right now all he cares about is being fucked past the point of oblivion.

A Drake comes in his mouth and he swallows greedily. Someone comes on his face, and he blinks away the sting, feeling it slide messy and hot down his face. Five minutes later, someone grabs his hair and yanks him close, coming on his lips, rubbing the head over them and forcing his come inside.

None of them taste like the real Drake, but he's past caring. It's *fine*.

Someone grabs his leg and lifts it up at an angle, and one of the cocks inside his ass slides in so deep he chokes. He has a dick in each hand, one rubbing against his face, two stretching his mouth wide, and someone pets his hair and tells him he's such a *good boy*. A mouth seals over his cock just as someone slides into his ass just right, and his tenth orgasm is dry, weak, and leaves him boneless and trembling.

He's done. He's pretty sure he's done, and he taps out, pounding the ground in a familiar rhythm he'd set up with Drake years ago. One of the hands brushes the hair back from his face, and Drake's voice cuts through the haze of deep rasping voices, ordering, "Put him down, he's had enough."

Too damn right he's had enough, Shane thinks dizzily. His

stomach turns and almost rebels at the amount of come he's swallowed, a fact that makes him feel filthy and used. Horny, and like he totally needs a shower.

For the first time in what feels like days, the last person slides out of his ass, and he's empty. That's such a relief that he lets out a sob, stumbling to the ground until Drake's arms—the real one, he's more sure than he ever has been about anything—come up to catch him.

"Shh. I've got you, you were so good. God, I love watching you." Long fingers pet his hair gently, holding him steady on his feet. "Want to see who was in you the whole time?"

I want to sleep for a dozen years, Shane thinks dizzily, but nods. Slowly, the other Drakes in the room melt away, puffing into smoke that doesn't linger. Shane turns his aching neck, and his eyebrows raise. "Huh. Never knew I was such a narcissist."

The other Shane smirks at him. The resemblance is uncanny, especially when it comes to the facial expressions. "Figured I could give you a little something back, as long as you were helping me burn it off."

The sense of the Fire Queen is no less dangerous now. Shane sobers slightly. At least he's full up on magic again, even if he feels like his skeleton was constructed out of battered wax and matchsticks. "Doesn't feel like you burned too much off, if you don't mind my saying so."

"But it *was* fun."

"And fun to watch," Father Aaron adds, stepping out of a shadowy corner.

Shane freezes. His eyes track slowly to the priest, watching him walk in rumpled robes. There are dark circles under his eyes and he looks distinctly ruffled. He looks like the very act of being in the same room with all of them causes him no small amount of physical pain, and as far as Shane can see, pays no attention to the two priests standing motionless against the other wall.

The Fire Queen burns off her disguise, transforming from

Shane to the visage that he knows so well, draped in constantly moving gold and green. Her smile is less of a smirk, and more something sad. "Do not hate the blackened man, Child of Flame. He deserves your pity."

"Blackened man?" Shane asks, raising an eyebrow. "The robes?"

Father Aaron shakes his head, and moves suddenly as quick as a striking snake, grabbing Drake's sword from the ground. "You asked me once," he tells Drake, leveling the sword at him with every look of a man who knows how to use it, "what you would see if you cut me open. It doesn't affect humans. Those that have gone nonhuman bleed in the custom of their race, don't they, Champion?"

"Not sure you should call me that anymore," Drake says hoarsely. At some point, he'd yanked his pants on, and Shane is somewhat envious of the protection he's got. Somehow he *always* ends up in these battles naked.

"You give up your post?"

"It's the Church that turned on me, Father. Not the other way around."

Father Aaron looks at Father Thomas and Father Douglas. "Them? Release your mind magic, they won't bother you."

"Why should we believe that?" Shane demands. "They tried to kill me. While I was naked!" This adds to the defense, he's certain. "And they shot up my place. I haven't even paid this month's rent yet, and now I'm not even gonna get my safety deposit back."

"They were doing as I told them."

The look on Drake's face is about equivalent to the way he'd looked when a nine-foot statue had come to life and punched him in the gut a few years ago. Shane can't even work up the bile necessary to say *I told you so*. "But… why?"

"Told you he wanted to get into your pants," Shane says. He listens with one ear, most of his energy going to the spells he's setting up. The Fire Queen shoots him a look—she knows what he's doing, sure enough, but she doesn't make a move to stop him and she certainly could if she wanted to.

"*You.*"

Shane hadn't honestly expected the depth of the anger directed suddenly his way. He backs up a step, blinking at the sudden venom in Father Aaron's voice as the priest advances on him. "I kept quiet. They told me to. Father Alice said you'd be a benefit in the long run, but she was wrong back then, and she's wrong now."

Back then probably means ten years ago, when Father Alice had first recruited Drake. Shane isn't sure why he can't shake the memory of meeting Father Aaron much longer ago than that, in a half-buried memory. He shifts closer to Father Aaron, seeking that clarity of memory that comes with being close to the sword, but it's still muddled, still in place.

He takes a deep breath, and a huge step forward, until the tip of the sword rests against his chest.

"Shane! Stop it!"

Shane remembers.

~

"What's your name?"

"Shane."

"Hi, Shane. I'm Father Alice. Can you stand up for me?"

A middle-aged woman in long black robes takes his hand. Hers is cool to the touch, the way everyone who isn't family is cool to the touch. Shane climbs unsteadily to his feet, swaying a little as his legs buckle.

"Whoa, easy there. How long have you been here?"

Shane doesn't look around. He knows there are bodies all over the room. The monster who'd murdered all of them had made sure of that. "Dunno." It feels like it's been a month, but he'd probably have gotten thirsty before then. Maybe it's more like a day, or a few hours.

She pats his head reassuringly. Shane hates it when people do that, like he's some kind of kid when he's almost eleven. He's already caught and passed Liam and Emma in age. Someday, he'll be sixteen like Melinda. "Did you see the thing that did this?"

"Yeah." Shane isn't sure he'll ever be able to stop seeing it. "A big monster. Bigger than a dragon."

"You've seen dragons?"

"I know Menteauxe and Threameauxe. They're my dad's friends, but they don't like me very much." None of his parents' friends do, really.

"Father Alice," a man says, harried and annoyed, "why are you talking to him? You know we're just going to have to—"

The woman holds up a stern hand. "I don't want to hear talk like that. He's been through enough."

"He's going to bring her down on us, on all of us! If not her, then that brother she calls a husband!"

"Gross," Shane says faintly, retreating to stand with his back against the wall.

Father Alice (Shane is pretty sure that Fathers are supposed to be boys, but he doesn't know too much about priests) glares at the man. "Aaron, get your head out of your ass. He's a child. We don't kill children."

"We don't know he's really a child," Aaron argues. "He's probably just fire-wrapped in flesh like the rest of us. Half of the skeletons here look like children, and you *know* the Connells have lived here for almost a hundred years."

"You know that isn't true. Feel him." Father Alice grabs Shane's arm—ow—and Aaron's, forcing him to grab. "Flesh and bone and blood. If you don't trust my instincts, at least trust your own."

Aaron tugs at his collar, visibly distressed. "What do you want to do with him? He just annihilated a Winter Serpent! A thousand men with flamethrowers—a thousand *Mages* couldn't manage that! Father Alice, there's no way the Connells could have a child that was anything other than an abomination. They *can't* just procreate, you know that."

Father Alice shrugs. "I'm thinking foster care."

"You've lost your mind."

"Do you want anyone getting your hands on power like this? The Ice King would wipe out half the world looking for him. The Fire Queen… well, she'd probably want to kiss his little face, but put the two of them together and kaboom."

"And your solution is foster care."

"Well," Father Alice says, running a hand through Shane's hair, and he starts to forget the noise the Winter Serpent made when he'd killed it, "not *just* foster care."

~

Fear pounds in Shane's blood with every pump of his heart. He knows it's not real, it just comes from some instinct he has reacting to Father Aaron, to the sword resting against his chest. "You haven't aged a day," he says quietly. "You were there. You all made it disappear, right?"

"Every huge organization specializes in making things disappear," Father Aaron says. His hand is surprisingly steady on the sword's hilt for someone who looks like hell. "We should have made you disappear forever. I knew you'd cause trouble. Knew it was you the second I heard about you, the Ice King's Vassal that never froze."

"Father Aaron." Drake's voice is raw and sad, and Shane could cheerfully kill the priest just for making his boyfriend sound like that. "You don't have to do this. He's not hurting anyone, you're a good person, I know you are."

"I'm a fool." Father Aaron smiles, and his wrist turns on the blade. It pricks into Shane's flesh, and that *stings*. He doesn't dare look down to see if there's blood, terrified that everything he's ever known has been just one more lie. Across the room, the Fire Queen blazes bright when his skin parts. "I thought I could get rid of what I am. Do you want to see what happens when I take the blade to my own flesh, Champion?"

Drake sounds broken. "Not anymore."

Shane could have told him it's too late. Father Aaron drags his arm across the sword, splitting the flesh with the subtle edge. Instead of immediately resealing itself after, as Drake's flesh had, a raw black wound opens. The closest thing Shane has ever seen to what comes crumbling out of him is damp charcoal, ground to a brittle edge.

Father Aaron looks down at the wound, fascinated. "It doesn't do this with any other blade," he informs them. "Just this one. But you, Shane Connell… your fire isn't out. No one slit you open and changed what you are."

"I'd kind of like to keep it that way," Shane says honestly, and backs up when Father Aaron advances on him again. "Why do you want me dead so bad? I kill the *bad* guys, I swear! I mean, I do it for money, but they're still bad and dead!"

"We try." The smile on Father Aaron's face is unbalanced at best. "We try to be something other than we are. I tried for years to unmake myself, but she calls, in the end, and even a prosthetic foot has to dance when the music plays."

"I'm not sure that's the metaphor you're looking for," Shane says, voice soothing, "but sure." He darts a glance over at the Fire Queen, merrily burning through a circle in the floor and hovering in midair. "Great. Uh, a little help? I know you aren't afraid to get close to me, not after that display."

Father Aaron shoves the point of the sword under Shane's neck, forcing him back against the wall. "Why are you calling her over? Do you want so badly to die?"

"Dude, she was inside me like ten minutes ago, I'm not scared to be close to her."

"She's dying." Father Aaron doesn't spare a glance back to the Fire Queen, who stands as still as a creature like her ever could, watching the two of them sadly. "Or exploding. Without the Ice King to keep her in check, she'll burn until she consumes even herself. If she doesn't check that flame, that is—and who is it who keeps letting her burn it off?"

"You… you're *not* working with her? You *want* her to die?" Shane asks, looking from the Priest to the Queen and back again. "I thought you were one of hers, one of… one of us?"

"I had that part of myself ripped away." Father Aaron's face is a rictus of pain and longing for something lost. "She came to me night after night, decades ago. God, we burned bright together."

"I never forgot," she whispers.

"But they kill everything. I couldn't help it. Sometimes the flames got too much, got out of control, and innocent people died." Father Aaron doesn't seem to notice the tears on his own face. Shane decides not to mention them. "The stronger she got, the stronger *he* got. They would rule our world if we let them."

"You're not wrong," the Fire Queen says unapologetically. "I am what I have become. If my fire spreads, I have nothing but more flames to add. My brother husband is or was fond of domination, and I lead and follow, as he leads and follows."

"Then…" Shane looks from Father Aaron to the Fire Queen, confused. "Wouldn't you *want* her to burn it off?"

"I want her to burn up." The gleam in the priest's eye is back. "I want her to consume every bit of fuel she has, gorged until there's nothing left to consume. Then, she'll know what it is to be snuffed out."

Shane eyes the Fire Queen. "You don't seem too put out by this."

She blinks. "Should I be?"

"He wants you dead."

"If I am dead, why should I care? I won't know I was snuffed."

"And if we leave you alive?"

That voice is Drake's. Shane had almost forgotten, and his eyes widen when he sees that Drake has grabbed one of the priest's guns, and is holding it like he knows how to use it (despite Shane being pretty sure Drake has never used a machine gun). He has it trained on Father Aaron, even though it looks like it costs him something to do that. "If we let you live, what then?"

She smiles, and flares through the ceiling, a puff of flame that leaves debris in its wake. "I am what I must be, Champion. The Child of Flame knows how difficult it is to bring the blaze under control."

There'd been almost no difference before and after Shane had been nailed six ways from Sunday, something he remembers with a wince. The Fire Queen hadn't felt like this before, not when he'd met her, still in the Ice King's service. Forget natural disasters—she feels like a nuclear bomb about to detonate.

"You need him around. The Ice King."

"He keeps me in check. We grow, though. When we both thrive, we grow."

"Then... why are you here?"

Her face softens. She looks sad, as much as a living flame made female can. "I... you remind me of them. If this must be, I'd rather be here to watch it. I hate the thought of dying apart from the last child of my kind."

In that second, Shane sees it. He sees the bloody warfare, the Ice creatures and Fire beings attacking each other, melting and freezing and wreaking havoc. He sees the countless deaths, the knowledge that at least they aren't proper Children, just creations or allies.

And he feels, when the Fire Queen looks at him, just how much it would pain her to lose him. Vaguely, he wonders if the Winter Serpent had caused the Ice King that sort of pain when he'd killed it.

It isn't hard to imagine a world filled with fire. Drake dying, the city burning, the oceans boiling. The last of humanity would be the Mages, but they would die as well. None of them are as strong as Shane is. None of them can do what he can do.

At least, what he hopes he can do.

It isn't as bad, this time. At least this time, Shane has a few moments to smile at Drake, to say a few words of love and let him know that in his mind, it's always been forever.

"Stop." Drake's face is aghast. He knows. "Father Aaron—"

"I can't stop, Champion. It has to be done."

"I know." Drake bows his head, then lifts it, grief and anguish in his face. "Let me do it."

The only way to fight fire when Ice is gone, Shane knows, is with fire. The rest of those like Father Aaron are gone, turned to dust inside or murdered by the Ice King. The dragons gave up their flame. Drake takes the sword, and Father Aaron lets him.

"I'd do it for you if I could," the priest says, speaking to Shane instead of Drake. "I'd take it into myself. A match once blown out can't be struck again."

Shane sees the ruse on Drake's face before he can follow it through. Drake is going to turn on Father Aaron. He'll rip him open, shout for Shane to do it *now*, and be certain that Shane will find some magic, some way to force the life back into him. Drake is sure, so *sure* that Shane can get them out of this, that for a second, Shane almost believes it. "You're such an asshole for believing in me," he says ruefully, and lunges forward without warning, impaling himself on the sword.

Everything is fire.

~

Interlude

~

120

In his dreams, Shane is nine years old, and Melinda is sixteen. She teaches him how to avoid the sight of humans, "and more importantly, other Mages."

"Why would I want to avoid them?"

"Shane," she'd said urgently, "you're not a Mage. It's just what we put down so they wouldn't take you away."

"So who wouldn't?"

"The… you know. Hospitals and stuff. Mom had to go when you were born, because all the Mages are scared of us."

Shane frowns. "Why didn't they have to go when you were born?"

Melinda laughs and tugs on his nose. "Dummy. Everyone knows what I am."

"And me?"

"Well…" She beams. "That's what makes you so special!"

Then Dad comes home, and Mom flies in an hour later. If nothing else, Shane knows who his parents are. That's probably enough.

~

Chapter Seven

~

Drake has always thought of fire as kind of a dirty thing. Not in a sexual way, though of course the terminology of fire as being "hot" is something, but in more of a physical way. It always leaves ash, soot, and jagged edges.

The fire that sweeps through the apartment building leaves nothing.

When a fire is hot enough, it leaves no smoke. If the wood is aged and dry, there's rarely anything left behind.

The police had already been en route when the fire started. They'd come for the sound of machine guns, a sound that had been reported five minutes earlier. Drake isn't sure whether something had stopped time in that apartment when the Fire Queen had arrived, or whether his former neighbors had simply been delinquent about making phone calls to the authorities. It doesn't matter. When the cops show up, there's nothing but the foundations of the building. The stone around it, Drake notices for the first time, is white, scoured clean by a fire so hot that a patch of sand is now a patch of glass.

"They said there was a fire," one cop says, frowning and scratching the back of his neck. "Begging your pardon, Mr. Young, but I don't see any smoke."

"Must have been a false alarm."

"You know, calling the cops out here for a false alarm can get you charged with a crime." The cop hesitates, then asks, "What happened to the building?"

"I don't know, officer," Drake says placidly. "It must have been a false alarm."

The cop writes something down, muttering to himself and squinting suspiciously at Drake before walking away to confer with his comrades.

"I could have handled that better," Shane says breezily from behind him.

"Yeah, but you're not here," Drake says, not turning to look. "Unless you want to get arrested for public nudity again. How many times would that be now?"

"Six? Seven. Probably seven." Shane speaks quietly, leaning against the mostly closed door of their neighbor's apartment.

"Your own fault. You should have grabbed a pair of pants before exploding the building."

"If I only had a nickel for every time I heard that."

Suddenly, Shane curses. Drake casts another glance at the cops before moving to his side, stepping out of their line of sight. "What is it? What's wrong?"

Shane looks like he's about to put his fist through the wall. "I had most of our rent in those jeans. I *liked* those jeans."

Drake rolls his eyes, and cups Shane's chin in one hand, drawing him in for a kiss. "You like any jeans that make your ass look good."

"All jeans make my ass look good, I have a great ass. I like jeans that make *everything* look good."

Drake laughs, and Shane collapses sideways onto him, looping long arms around his neck in the shadow of the doorway. "All that," he says ruefully, "and I still wind up looking like a refugee. This time we don't even have your place to go back to."

"Father Alice will put us up," Drake says confidently, and Shane sighs.

"I guess. I can always make a living exterminating ants."

Drake leans his head against Shane's. Someday, a long time after he stops smelling fire, his heart might stop pounding. It's impossible to remember the sick crunch of flesh meeting steel when Shane had lunged forward. Drake had felt the shock reverberate up his entire arm, had started to scream, and the fire had roared up in an absolute plume, engulfing everything around them.

Then it had cleared as soon as it had manifested, leaving Father Douglas, Father Thomas, and Shane all unconscious on the foundations of the apartment building. The complexes on either side had been untouched, a fact that Drake doesn't even want to think about explaining. The priests hadn't said a word when they'd awakened, just taken one look at each other and cleared out before the police had arrived.

And Shane, the man Drake would give his life for a hundred times over, had looked like an unblemished angel. Drake had found the sword next to him, bloodlessly clean, scoured by the same flames that had wiped their building off the map.

Drake brushes the hair gently back from Shane's face. "You remember stuff now?"

"I don't know." A corner of Shane's mouth turns up, then relaxes. "Not sure I want to remember everything. I mean… if something else big happens, sure, but otherwise, I'd rather just make our lives together." What those lives will be when they don't have money, prospects, or a place to live might not be entirely certain, but that doesn't bother either of them. It hadn't stopped them when they were seventeen, and it isn't going to stop them now. If anything, there's always, always work for bounty hunters, whether the Church still wants Drake or not.

"Even not knowing?" Knowing what he is, knowing what his family is, knowing what he's born from might be something of a detriment to most people. Then again, for all Drake knows, Shane had gotten his answers in that moment of blinding light. It wouldn't be the weirdest thing he's seen all day.

But whatever Shane had seen or hadn't seen, whatever he knows or doesn't, he seems to want to cling to Drake's neck and kiss him. That's most of what Drake requires in a partner, if he's being honest.

Shane punches him wearily. "I know everything I need to know."

"You hit like a four-year-old."

"Fuck off, I just eviscerated myself."

"Not very well," Drake points out, and pokes Shane in the belly. "I knew those idiots didn't know what they were talking about."

It's a lie, and they both know it. The sword had gone through his skin, and even if he hadn't bled, something had come out.

Sometimes, the lie is more important than a truth that could bring both of them down.

"Do you still feel her?" Drake asks, because he has to. "When you do the thing with the fire?"

Shane shakes his head. "No more than I feel him." By mutual understanding, they don't use the names. "I don't know if they're dead or recovering or banished or what, but they're not here."

"And we are."

"Yeah."

"So… we win."

Shane laughs, and sags gratefully against Drake's chest. "I guess we do."

"And the next time something comes out of the darkness to pick a bone with what you are…"

"You have the sword." Shane shrugs. "And I am what I am, whatever that is."

"My partner."

Shane looks up at him, fingers lacing tight around his neck. "Yeah. That'll do."

~